conversations
with
magic
stones

conversations
with
magic
stones

mark
blayney

Mark Blayney
5.9.04

manuscript

First published 2003
by Manuscript Publishing
41 Southview Road
Marlow
Bucks
SL7 3JR

Copyright © Mark Blayney 2003

Holy and Raw was first published in *Signals: 3*, London Magazine Editions 2000. This collection © Mark Blayney 2003.

Extract from *Dream Story* by Arthur Schnitzler translated by J.M.Q. Davis reproduced by permission of Eric Glass Ltd.

The extracts from Ovid's *Metamorphoses* are from the 1575 translation by Arthur Golding.

All rights reserved. No part of this publication may be reproduced, stored or transmitted in any form without prior permission in writing from the publisher except for the purposes of review or fair dealing for academic study. This book may not be lent, resold or otherwise circulated in any form of binding or cover other than that in which it is published.

This book is a work of fiction. The views and ideas expressed within it should not be regarded as the opinions of the author or of the publisher. All characters are fictional and any similarity to any actual person, living or dead, is coincidental. The moral right of the author has been asserted (Copyright, Designs and Patents Act 1988).

It is the publisher's policy to use paper manufactured from sustainable forests.

British Library Cataloguing in Publication Data
A CIP record for this book is available from the British Library.

ISBN 0 9545505 0 1

Printed and bound by The Cromwell Press, Trowbridge, Wiltshire.
Cover design by Anna Mullin.

For Hannah

contents

paean 7
translations 39
conversations with magic stones 67
in shape of lions 87
holy and raw 145
masque 163

paean

I

On a bridge, a black smudge resolved itself as a woman in a long coat. I rubbed my glasses but the rain still hung in front of my eyes. My view warped and blurred as I moved my head. The black smudge, an oily thumbprint now on the wet canvas of the painted bridge, moved slightly. I wiped my glasses again on my sleeve, and put them back on. The woman seemed to be waving at me. The hand flickered, disappeared and re-appeared as it moved across the thin, uneven surface of glass that connected me to the world.

I took my glasses off to clean them for a third time, the world swirling across my weak retinae like soapy water being sucked towards a plughole. As the world refocused, at last less wet and distorted, I looked towards the bridge. The girl had gone. Hunched in his kiosk, a man with a wet cigarette.

I lit my own wet cigarette when sheltered by the statue of van Eyck, and slowly walked the last few yards to the hotel. In the spotless empty room, the maid had put my lens cleaner in the ashtray. I put it in my back pocket, criticising myself for forgetting it.

That night in the bar Ceris bemoaned how the weather was even worse than at home. I sat looking at the barstool, wondering why it exercised such fascination over me. Ceris bought another round of drinks. I asked her for a Campari and she paused before going. I caught her eye and shrugged. 'It's what I feel like,' I said. I had no idea why I wanted it. She narrowed her eyes and smiled in reply, and went to the bar.

Eventually we fell back into the hotel room and made love listening to the rain sliding down the long slim windows. I did not tell Ceris about the girl on the bridge.

II

At breakfast, Ceris was on form and I, as usual, was silent. The hotel insisted entirely of English couples. I shook my head. *Consisted* entirely of English couples.

We were the youngest there. Ceris was spooning honey onto her roll and chatting amiably with the couple on the next table about Antwerp, which we had visited the previous day. 'It was raining of course,' Ceris was saying, 'but somehow Rubens' house looked more, I don't know, more beautiful in the wet. But you wouldn't believe how long it took us to find it. We came out of Antwerp station and you looked at a map and got it hopelessly wrong, didn't you darling, and we got lost, and we asked in several shops and do you know no one knew where Rubens' house was, and in two of the shops the staff even went, "Who?"'

Kathy, forkful of ham en route to her mouth, gasped. 'You're joking.'

'No. And we tried to get a taxi and there weren't any taxis, and we went all the way down these escalators to get a tram and none of the trams said where they were going, they just had funny girls' names and things, so we thought well, we won't know where to get off, and there were no buses, so we walked, and then it started to rain and we felt so hungry we went to have a McDonald's and do you know it was actually quite nice, it wasn't like McDonald's at home.'

'You must forgive my friend,' I said. 'She's not very chatty this morning. It must be the change in climate.'

Ceris slapped my arm. Kathy pursed her lips. Her husband Martin laughed in a low, growly manner like a dog pulling a toy with its mouth. He ate a piece of Gruyere thoughtfully, waiting for the women to continue, not interested in being part of the conversation himself.

'What was Rubens' house like?' asked Kathy. She wiped crumbs from her mouth with a shiny white napkin.

'Oh it was lovely. Really lovely,' Ceris nodded enthusiastically. 'Although,' she qualified, 'there weren't many pictures by Rubens.'

Martin, digesting a piece of salami, choked, covered his mouth, went red, waved his hand in front of his face. Ceris looked at him, a wide eyed, bland smile on her face. 'Is your husband all right?' she asked Kathy in a low voice.

'I'm fine,' said Martin, making his face straight.

'And, have you tried to go out to dinner yet?' said Ceris, veering from one subject to another with much the same sense of enthusiasm and surprise as when she changed motorway lanes.

'Er – '

'Everywhere just serves steak or scampi. It's ridiculous.'

'We were surprised that the hotel doesn't have its own restaurant.'

'Well exactly.'

I got up and, unnoticed, slipped back to the hotel room. When Ceris came back I was dozing.

The morning was clear but cold. In an ice blue sky, huge floating clouds like icebergs sped from one horizon to another, moving hurriedly to keep themselves warm. We walked past the canal, past van Eyck, past the restaurant where last night we had looked at each other in stunned amazement when the owner announced at 9.30 that he was not serving food any more. All the other restaurants were closing too. We ended up having a pizza in our room, thanks to the friendly efforts of the girl on reception.

We walked a little further along the road to the corner before crossing, in order to walk on the squares of rubber set into the pavement so that blind people would know they were at the edge of the road. 'Why can't all the pavements be made of rubber?' asked Ceris. It would make walking so much less exhausting.' She squeezed my hand. I put my arm round her.

III

'Where do you stand on mysticism?'

Belgian countryside panned flatly by from the privileged height of the sleek, smooth and more impressively, punctual train.

'Be more specific,' I said, resting my head on my hand. You had to be patient with Ceris when she was one of her leading questions moods.

Ceris shrugged, unintimidated. 'Your thoughts,' she said.

'Your feelings, impressions. What you think.'
I scratched my cheek and puffed my cheeks out in what Ceris calls my hamster impression. 'Mysticism is by definition illogical. There is just the unexplained. If something supposedly mystical exists at all, it is real – it can be explained by science – it just hasn't been yet.'
'*What?*'
'Electricity was mystical before we found out what it was and what its properties were. Sailors saw this thing they called St. Elmo's Fire, and were afraid of it. Now we know it's electricity forming around rigging. Reasonable explanation – science just hadn't explained it at the time, so it became mystical. As soon as it's explained, it's not mystical any more.'
She considered this. The train pulled quietly into Ghent. 'You don't believe in it then.'
'I believe in things that exist, but then you don't need to believe in them – because they exist.'
'Isn't that a tautological statement?'
'Only because you want a definition of what I 'believe'. Telepathy, for instance. I neither believe in it nor don't believe in it. I have no opinion either way. It might exist, it might not. I have no evidence that it does, but then no evidence that it doesn't. I'm open-minded. But if it does exist, it will be explainable by science and thus not be mystical. If it exists, it exists. Nothing mysterious in that. If there can never be an explanation for it, then no, it doesn't exist; so it isn't 'mystical' either, it's just fictional.'
Through the noisy chatter of American tourists and backpackers with silly little beards, we descended into the station and out into the fresh spareness of the city. We followed the crowd, trusting them to take us to the trams, and the crowd proved correct. No single mind led the crowd; it somehow found its desti-

nation by group will. Ceris bought the tram tickets, which like every other local bus and tram ticket were 40f each.

As the tram heaved and rolled through the streets Ceris rubbed a hand thoughtfully across the silk hood of her hair. 'So do you believe in God then?' she asked. A woman on the next seat glanced up at us.

I looked out at the glass squares of the shops drifting blankly past. 'I'm inclined not to believe in God,' I said, feeling the pale sun on my face.

'Why not?'

'I don't see any evidence for it.'

The tram mawed violently to the left and two unwary pedestrians leapt back onto the pavement as if their film had been run backwards.

'Isn't the evidence all around you?'

'No. It's all accidental. There was a random chemical accident and it led to this. Put two chemicals together and all sorts of strange things will happen. Given billions of years, I don't find worlds and animals particularly surprising.'

She whistled. 'I find all that pretty hard to take. How can beings just have come out of nothing?'

'How can God just have come out of nothing?' I stared into the granite street, peopled by random people wandering back and forth. Shards of light and ghosts of faces flashed on the window as it turned a corner and reflected passengers and the sun.

'Well – he just did.'

'So why is it impossible that we 'just did?'

She thought about this.

'All accidental,' I said, 'and when we die we vaporise.'

In the back of the coach two babies cried out into the emptiness of the coach because they didn't know why they were there and didn't know what all the noise was. Their mothers tried to quieten them but could not stop them wailing. Neither could the coach, which rocked back and forth, trying to convince its inhabitants they were back in the womb, warm and safe. The infants still screamed. They did not know what was happening to them and no one could give them good reasons why they had to be cooped up in such a strange, dizzying, moving world. I looked out of the window. It was starting to rain again and I felt instinctively in my pocket for my lens cleaner.

IV

Ghent cathedral, solid and squat in the grey light, looked like a hunched, sleeping giant. In an alcove dug into the beast's claw were the bronze statues of four men, stained the same pale green as van Eyck. I looked more closely at the statues, surprised to see that one of them was a slightly paler green than the others. How could it be? Had they started to clean them, and this one had been first?

Ah, I suddenly thought –

The statue moved. It raised a clublike, metallic hand. Ceris jumped and gave an involuntary little squeal. The hand turned and showed its stained, creased palm. We now noticed that there was a small group of people standing around watching; at first glance we had thought they were just part of the endless stream of people milling around the cathedral. The man produced an elegant mime, looking uncertainly at the other statues, mimicking their impressions, holding his streaky green cap out for coins. People smiled and clapped. Ceris gave him all her change. He nodded slowly, raised his bronze eyebrows to her, slowly opened his mouth and cracked a green-toothed smile.

We took a boat trip on the canal, saw a dire performance of Mozart's *Requiem* in the cathedral – just three statues outside now, it didn't seem complete – and then went to eat. Whilst looking out for a suitable restaurant, Ceris nervously glanced several times at her watch, even though it was not yet eight o'clock. We peered into the tiny windows of one particular restaurant, which steamed up in anticipation of our entering. It offered a wide variety of steaks and also scampi.

'Let's try somewhere else,' said Ceris.

We walked over the bridge and looked down on the canal. Lights shimmered and winked at us from the black water, like a pool of ink being fondled by a brush. On the other side, another restaurant crouched alluringly in the dark, its green and blue neon interior shining dimly like the skin of some Amazonian frog. We walked over. The menu was propped up against the door, and in the darkness I had to squat down to read it properly. I compared the many different types of steak available, then became aware of a gasp behind me, and of Ceris talking to someone.

'My goodness, you shouldn't do that, you startled me.'

It was one of those moments where many things happen within a fraction of a second. I turned round and saw a tableau of Ceris cowering slightly, with her hand to her throat and another arm stretching blindly towards me; and the silhouetted shape of someone standing next to her. Before I had fully registered this, I was standing up. Before I had fully stood up, the black shape resolved itself into an unshaven man of about fifty. I noticed a red mark on his forehead; he shrank back from us. He tipped his head in an acknowledgement of me and in apology. I realised that he hadn't seen me to begin with and had thought Ceris was on her own. A second had passed now. As I started to frown, he raised a hand towards me. I thought, what time is it, it's only eight o'clock. Ceris shrunk into me and touched the collar of my coat. I felt the back of her hand rub on my throat. I glanced at her, then back at the man. On a sudden gust of wind I smelt the alcohol on him. Nearly a second and a half had now passed. Ceris's initial words to the man were still echoing in my head.

He remained where he was, vulnerable and frightened. He scratched his cheek. 'I didn't, er, I didn't...' he said. Fear evaporated from Ceris and mutated into anger. 'You frightened me!' she said.

The man started to wheeze. I wondered if he was ill. My shoulders relaxed and I saw light in his eyes. I felt sorry for him. I had formed 'are you okay?' in my mind, but not yet said it, when he started to reach out. He reached towards Ceris's neck, and the wheeze turned into a guttural, breathy sigh. Ceris tensed up, leant backwards. Sinews in my body woke up. My arms and legs seemed to raise into the air.

'Right,' I said in an unnaturally clipped voice. I grabbed Ceris's hand with great force, whirled round, dragged her after me. 'Goodnight,' I said, not turning my head but speaking in a sufficiently loud voice for him to hear. 'Bye. Enjoy your evening.' I marched Ceris across the length of the bridge, staring ahead, and did not slow down until we reached the other side.

We fell into another restaurant, brightly lit, where we had white wine and scallops and veal. We felt the day fall from us like heavy clothes being cast off. By the time we got the train back, we were both giggling and hugging each other and dozing. The train glided smoothly through the night.

V

In the Groëninge Museum, I gazed at Bosch's *Last Judgement*. I saw Ceris, reflected in the painting's protective glass, gazing with me. The painting caught her and held her like a fly in its oily, intricately painted web. 'I've never seen anything like it,' she murmured. Next to me I heard a tinny, disembodied voice emerge from a hand-held audio guide and tell its disinterested holder all about Bosch and his work. The holder stared at the centre panel, his eyes unmoving, his face unmoved, and when the guide told him to, he walked away.

The faces of the damned looked blankly at us. Toads, owls and snakes crawled symbolically in every corner. I noticed how Heaven blended into Earth, which blended into Hell across the triptych. I pointed it out to Ceris. 'That's very unusual. Normally the three places are separate, distinct.'

Ceris nodded without paying too much attention to the painting. 'Well yes. They would be, wouldn't they?'

The museum was closing as we staggered out into the fading light. Alongside the canal a group of six musicians in shabby greys and blacks played the first movement of Brahms' first string sextet. I stood for a moment with Ceris, watching them, or perhaps we were standing by a Bruges museum in the trickling rain, and this was the soundtrack to our film.

Through the archway of the Gruithuis Museum the bronzes and oranges of the ancient brick building glimmered in the afternoon light. We walked through the archway just to stand there, soak it up. A kind of creeper thatched the roof opposite, dark vibrant red like wine, turning quickly into a rich forest green. I had the urge to climb up and taste it, smell it, run it through my fingers. It was as much as I could do not to hop up and down on the spot thinking about it. I rubbed my hand across Ceris's back and sank my head onto her shoulder, licking her neck and rubbing my nose in her hair. She smelled of autumn. She hugged me, familiar now with these strange outbursts.

We went into a restaurant and I thirstily drank two large Hoegaardens before the food arrived. It was steak, but I didn't really care what it was. I ate ravenously, impolitely, holding my glass up to a passing waiter to indicate more beer while still chewing. For once Ceris listened and I talked – about the iconography in the Groëninge's paintings, how everything you saw had a meaning and a symbolism, but these days most people ignore this and just see the paintings as paintings. Ceris said it was okay to look at them just as paintings, and I said of course, of *course* it is as long as you still enjoy them, as long as you still appreciate them. But most people don't appreciate them, and the reason for that is that they look at a painting and see a painting.

Outside it drizzled with rain. I stepped uncertainly into the afternoon light, which was bright from reflecting on the puddles in the road. The air smelt fresh and autumnal and the click of horses' hooves as they trotted past seemed louder than normal. Trees blew in the breeze and dropped leaves. Wind rippled across the top of the canal and confused the ducks, who buoyed along looking rather alarmed as they were swept towards the bank.

Ceris pointed to a little kiosk by the bridge. 'Shall we take a boat trip? Do you suppose we're too late? What time do you think they stop?' She ran ahead and chatted to the woman in the kiosk. I walked more sedately behind, feeling the drink slosh about in my stomach.

I walked unsteadily down the steps. By a squat wooden hut,

rain dripping from its roof, stood a tall, slightly stooping boat-keeper. He was about forty, with thin strands of blond hair clinging wetly to his forehead. Dull brown eyes the colour of the canal. He was wearing a waterproof jacket and waterproof trousers and was soaked to the skin. He stared glumly out from under the brim of his waterproof hat. I sat heavily on the cold metal bench and looked at the sky, still piercingly blue but with black lumpy clouds chugging along the horizon like smoke from a steam train.

Ceris asked him how long the next trip would be. He talked slowly with his hands sunk deep in his pockets. He looked mournfully at Ceris while she talked, nodding frequently and occasionally casting a damp glance towards me. A drop of water hung from the end of his nose. He tried to smile when Ceris laughed but his mouth wasn't really up to the job. Limp and tired, he resembled a dead trout at the bottom of a fisherman's bucket.

The boat arrived and the boatman raised his eyebrows. 'Ah,' he said, rubbing his nose. 'Here we are. Is my turn.' The man steering the boat got out and dripped onto the wooden quay. Nodding at the second man, who walked to the doorway of the hut and stood there staring blankly ahead like a sentry, our boatkeeper showed us to the boat and helped Ceris in. We waited for a few minutes; two other couples appeared and got in too.

The boat shuddered as it sped under the bridge. I looked down into the water and watched my unmoving reflection as everything else rushed about it. Sitting back and leaning against Ceris's warm body, I closed my eyes for a moment and breathed her in.

It started to rain heavily. I heard the other couples reach for the umbrellas in the pit of the boat. As I opened my eyes, the umbrellas opened like flowers coming into bud. We sailed along under a bright canopy of bobbing red and white. I could glimpse occasional green and brown flashes of buildings and walls, but mostly just saw umbrellas, shifting up and down like balloons rubbing against each other. Ceris stroked my head absently.

'Up ahead,' declared the boatman in a monotone, 'is smallest medieval window in Europe.' I looked up and between two umbrellas glimpsed a tiny, uninteresting window in a solid block of wall. Ceris and I looked at each other and shrugged. The boatman was pointing his long bony finger at the window, stabbing into the air to draw our attention to the insignificant object.

Half waking, half dozing, I sat and breathed in the air, drugged by black spewing diesel and the incessant mesmerising drone of the boatman's commentary. Some years later, the whine of the motor descended in pitch and we chugged back to where we had begun. 'This is the end of the tour,' intoned our guide, 'I hope it has been to your satisfaction. It is traditional to tip the guide. Thank you.'

We walked towards a restaurant, hugging each other and not saying much. Ceris kept looking at her watch anxiously. 'It's only half past six,' I reassured her.

'I mean,' murmured Ceris after another silence, 'the *largest* medieval window in Europe might have been interesting. But it was just a small hole cut in a wall. Why is a small window an achievement?'

The rain refused to leave off. Eventually we found an Indian restaurant – something of an achievement in Bruges – and flopped in. We had finally managed to sober up, so Ceris quickly ordered a bottle of red wine. The food was superb, the waiters astoundingly friendly – they couldn't understand why everyone else wanted to eat steaks and scampi either – and we wished we had discovered it sooner.

We walked back across the square, stumbling occasionally on the cobbles. 'These roads,' Ceris complained, 'are so uneven.'

'Yes,' I said, 'but the odd thing is, they're not so uneven when you're not drunk.'

'Yes,' said Ceris, 'yes, I'd noticed that.'

'Yes, me too.'

'Yes, and me.'

'That makes three of us.'

'Or is it four?' She tried to count on her fingers.

We rounded the corner and crossed the road, taking special care to walk on the rubbery bit of pavement. We walked past the Argentinian steak house. I pointed up to the 'men at work' sign. 'They make two little piles of rubble here,' I observed, 'not just one.'

'Yes,' said Ceris, 'and they wear a little hat as well.'

The canal gleamed blackly like ink. It did not ripple or make any sound. I leant over the side and could not imagine there was a bottom to it. If you fell in you would fall forever; it was like that place outside a black hole where to you, the whole of the future happens in a moment, but to outside observers you are frozen there, suspended in time forever.

VI

Above us, a clock ticked. It was cool in the bar, and so dark that several times I dropped my glass on the table with a thud, the table being further away than I had thought it was.

Ceris giggled. 'You're drunk.'

Conversations with Magic Stones

'No, I'm not,' I assured her. 'I'm clumsy.'

'Where are all the other English tonight?' This was addressed to the barman. He came rushing round from the other side of the bar, waving his arms, pleased at this apparent invitation to engage in conversation.

'I don't know where they all are this evening,' he mused thoughtfully. 'I am thinking to myself, perhaps they have gone out.'

'Yes, that's quite possible,' I replied, sipping my drink.

'Sometimes I think, why is it always English here? And then I think I know. It is because everyone here, they all speak English. The English, I think they don't speak other languages very much.'

'No, not very much, no.'

'While you come here, you speak English, everyone they speak English back to you.'

'Yes,' I riposted. I was tired and wanted to go to bed, and knew the barman would not leave us in peace. Ceris started talking to him, full of energy, full of interest in his wife and where he lived and how long he had worked here and whether he'd ever been to England and what his sons did and how old they were and where they lived and whether they were married and what their wives did.... It could go on infinitely. I felt, as I slowly slipped into a pleasant silent haze that was like being underwater, a love for her that was like reaching out to someone and not quite being able to touch, but it not mattering because the feeling was warm and comfortable and I could see the fingers, just out of reach but waggling in a friendly way, and I didn't have to make any effort, I could just lie there and imagine touching them, and I knew she would always be there, even if I never said another word.

Later, the English couples filtered in slowly and the barman enjoyed himself chatting to them, asking them how their days had been, and what they had been doing, and eventually, ultimately, pouring them drinks.

It neared midnight and I looked at Ceris. 'Shall we go to bed?' she asked. 'I'll just have one more drink,' she added before I had a chance to nod.

I glanced at the barman and he looked at me expectantly. I nodded and he started pouring our respective drinks. How unlike home. You could be drinking the same thing all evening and you would go to the bar and the disinterested girl would still say, 'Yes?' and blankly wait for you to tell her for the fifth time what you wanted.

The door opened and all eight of us craned round to see who it could be. Two people aged about thirty walked in. They were not English. How strange, we thought, to see foreigners here. We all looked at each other in slight consternation, at the concept of these aliens interrupting our cosy English gathering.

They looked round and beamed as if they knew us. We all wondered which couple knew the new arrivals. No one did. There was a pause, while we waited for them, and they waited for us. As if we all expected some signal or event. The barman hummed absently to himself and wiped an ashtray. The signal would not come from him; not for a long time anyway.

Gradually, time trundled on again and the man leant over to the barman, who was reading a matchbox, and asked for drinks. The girl ran a hand through her long hair. I took my glasses off and rubbed them on my shirt and put them back on again. The shirt did not clean them very well and I saw hazes of the girl and the bar when I moved my face. Thin lines of light like javelins shot across in front of me at oblique angles. The lights around the girl's head broke up into a prism and I saw several versions of her looking down on me.

The man saw me looking at the girl and nodded at me. 'This is Irena Marsalis,' he said proudly, significantly.

'Pleased to meet you,' I said.

He looked at me a little quizzically. The woman's face was motionless, impassive, waxy. 'No, I mean this is Irena *Marsalis*,' he said. He said it loudly, turning his face slightly while he did so, allowing the rest of the bar to hear.

'Is it,' I said, nodding.

'You haven't heard of Irena Marsalis?'

I shook my head. Slowly, seven other heads also shook.

The woman stayed entirely impassive and silent, but I detected the tiniest deflation in her features. She conspicuously shook her hair out like a horse self-consciously coming in second.

'Irena is very famous in Holland.'

'Oh,' said Ceris. Pause. 'I've never been to Holland,' she explained. Low guttural laughter from some invisible corner behind Kathy.

'Oh, it is very beautiful,' chipped in the barman, animated again if is someone had injected something into his arm. 'Well, some of it is. Flat, of course. I have found Rotterdam very interesting, and also – '

'Yes, well, Irena is very well known there,' said the man, steering the conversation back on course.

'What's your name?' I asked him.

'Me? Oh, I am only Dirk.'

VII

We all made ourselves at home in a little circle, and Ceris talked about someone else she'd once met who was famous but who she'd never heard of, so that was a bit of a coincidence, and Irena fluttered her eyelashes and rolled her eyes as she looked around the bar and sighed from time to time, and once she ran a hand over her forehead as if she had a headache.

'Are you all right?' I asked her.

'Oh yes,' she said. 'I find, you know, it very warm in here.'

'Oh, that will be the fire,' said the barman, coming forward helpfully. 'I will let this log burn and I will not replace it.'

'That's very thoughtful of you,' said Irena, smiling at him. He nodded, and scuttled back to his little hole.

'He's very obliging, isn't he?'

Irena looked at me. 'He is. He's a very pleasant person. But I think this about people. I look at you, for instance. For an example. Say I was in love with you.'

I paused with my drink halfway towards my mouth.

Irena laughed a kind of soundless, breath-intaking laugh, rolling her eyes slightly and clutching her hand to her chest. The hand had at least one ring on each finger, and moved up and down rapidly. 'I mean of course I cannot be, I have only just met you.'

'Yes.'

'But if I were in love with you, which I could be, I would think you to be a very kind and pleasant person.'

She gazed at me intently, blinking only occasionally. Her eyes, green and feline, were matt and opaque, as if they hid secrets, even though she was apparently looking openly at me. I could see myself reflected, frozen as if in a portrait with a glass of beer and with my shoulders stooping slightly as I looked at her. My body looked rounded and the room was circular in her eyes, as if it were a drawing in *Alice in Wonderland*, or the room in the mirror in the *Arnolfini Portrait*.

'You're a singer, I take it?' I said. She rolled her eyes a little. 'Yes, yes, I am a singer, is it my loud voice you have guessed by!' She slapped my knee. 'I am giving a concert in Brussels next week, you know.'

'Irena is very famous in Brussels too,' chipped in Dirk. Irena glanced back at him. He gulped at his beer. He was very sweaty and somewhat overweight, with a fringe of damp curly hair clinging to his pasty forehead and flabby jowls. The ensemble was completed with a boil.

Irena turned her attention back to me and leaned forward earnestly. 'You have a very beautiful girlfriend,' she said.

'Yes, she's wonderful. I don't know how she puts up with me sometimes.'

'You are difficult to put up with? You hit her?' Irena's famous loud voice echoed round the bar.

'No, no,' I said, mortified, looking round the bar, 'of course I don't hit her, what makes you think that?'

'Then what do you mean by you are difficult to live with?' Her mouth enlargened, the lips reddened; she became irresistible in a vaguely frightening way.

'You want a drink?' asked Dirk. Irena ignored him. She leant towards me again. The previously piercing voice lowered to a smoky mutter. 'He's worried you know, he thinks every man I meet I will go off with. Ha! You see, I am in love with someone else, who I cannot have. I am very sad. But I think everyone needs to have love, you know? You cannot sleep in a lonely bed. So I make do with him. He is easy, he does what I say, he doesn't cause scenes. I can't bear it when people cause scenes, can you? You like a cigarette?'

She touched my knee again and sat back in her chair, which creaked. I slowly shook my head as she lit a Marlboro, waved the match about her face as if performing an incantation, threw the burned wood with aplomb onto the floor, and sat considering me through spiralling clouds of blue smoke. She picked her glass up slowly and I thought she was going to perform a libation on me. I glanced at Ceris, who caught my eye and smiled tightly, then carried on talking to Kathy and Martin. All three of them spoke little and had their chairs angled towards us.

The bar was quiet as our audience eavesdropped. Irena half-opened her mouth. Her front teeth had a small gap between them. Something that should have been unattractive I found attractive. 'Yes,' she said, 'I am thinking to myself, this is a nice person.'

Dirk, finally tiring of this, got up. He stood for a second, silhouetted by the low greenish light from the bar. His body angled, changed shape. For a moment I thought he was going to hit me. Irena looked up at him, unalarmed, curious about what he would do. He loomed for a moment then looked around at the crowd, all staring in fascination from their various corners. Eventually he walked past me and stood in front of Ceris.

'What is your name?' he asked her.

'Hello. Um… Ceris.' She shot a slightly alarmed glance towards me.

He knelt in front of her and took her hand. 'Ceris, you are a very beautiful person.' He kissed her hand.

'Thank you.'

He nodded, moved slowly back to his chair, cleared his throat and sat down, pulling his trousers up as he did so. Irena languidly dropped ash on the floor and coughed. 'Well,' she murmured, circling the hand that held the cigarette. 'Anyway. You live in England?'

Dirk, having left a deliberate pause in which he found himself ignored, turned his gaze on Irena. His eyes swivelled in their sockets independently of the rest of the face, which stayed still.

'Drink?' he asked. Irena smiled at me, a flicker around her eyelids, and then said, 'Yes. Thank you. Campari.'

Somehow another beer had appeared in front of me. I didn't even remember finishing the last one. The room was starting to swim and Irena's smoke was giving me a headache. I looked towards Ceris, but my eyes had difficulty reaching her. Moving my glance towards her was like trying to crawl up huge steps, steps that were too large for me to clamber over. Steps as they would appear to a baby. Someone was saying something to me, but I couldn't work out what it wasor who was saying it.

I looked towards Irena. Her hair was a mass of red and brown, swirling like it was caught in the wind or underwater. I could see the edge of her face, the tip of her nose. The room behind her was hazy, grey-green, as if painted quickly and inaccurately in oils. The paintings on the wall hung at odd angles, the gilt of their frames liquid, the curls and waves embedded in the frame moving slightly, made of mercury or liquid gold.

I shook my head. Ceris was tugging at my shoulder, but I couldn't get up. People were standing, leaving, the room was breaking up. I shook my head. The *party* was breaking up. But it was true. The room was breaking up as well. The ceiling was lifting from the walls, the bar was sliding further away from the wall, the chairs were veering towards the door. I looked wildly at the doorway and saw Irena lift a heavy black coat down from the hook, which was moving slowly up and down the wall. She walked from the room, followed by the others who all swayed as if on a boat. I began to feel seasick.

Ceris helped me but she seemed to be impatient. Once I was on my feet she went ahead. I was the last left in the bar. I followed her and tried unsuccessfully not to make contact with the walls on my way out.

The corridor narrowed in on me, became thinner. The space ahead disappeared at its vanishing point; the ceiling descended and the floor sloped upwards and the walls converged. I knew I would not be able to crawl to the end of it, I would not fit; as it was I was having difficulty moving forwards, I was becoming too big for the space, I was Alice looking down the rabbit hole. I slumped against one wall, sat there, sweating, wondering what to do. I could still hear music from the bar echoing around my head; energetic classical music, Vivaldi on original instruments, getting louder and more frenetic and distorting, the ancient mandolins and hautbois somehow creating feedback and electrical interference.

Irena was kneeling in front of me, her black coat a shroud around her. She was leaning forward, showing me a palm, I could see the lines on her palm, she was saying something to me but it was just noise, vibrations in the air, a bow being drawn across an invisible string. She leaned forward and the space around me darkened. She removed my glasses and everything tipped upside down and merged, like the patterns of rainwater on a puddle of oil.

She leaned further forward and I smelt Campari. Her face loomed large, bulbous, unreal. The gap in her teeth and her green eyes and the flame red hair were all larger, exaggerated, distorted. She kissed me. The room got darker and her face became fuller and huger, until it blotted out the rest of my vision and became everything, and absorbed me.

VIII

'You were drunk.'

'I wasn't just drunk, there was something wrong with the wine, it was off, or I was drugged.'

'You were *what?!*'

'I was drugged, it felt like being drugged, one minute I was fine, the next minute I couldn't even speak.'

'It was drinking all day and then having wine and then asking for Campari for God's sake, what was that all about, and then having beer again – '

'I didn't ask for Campari – that was her – that was the other night I asked for it – '

'Oh, and I found these.' Her hand, blurred and shapeless, moved towards me. I fumbled and grasped and eventually felt my glasses. I groped along the familiar shape, held the sides, put them on and everything came into focus. They felt strange on my face; they had been bent out of shape.

'Where were they?'

'I found them in the corridor when I went down for breakfast. Kathy and Martin wondered if you were all right.'

'Oh yes... yes... fine...'

She looked at her watch. 'Well I'm going to have a shower. Then I think we should go. I thought we could do the cathedral today, or perhaps take the train to Ostende, that's only up the road. I wonder about Ostende, I mean it could just be a port, could be really boring. But these places you've heard of, you want to go to them, don't you?'

She walked over to me. 'Or how's your head?' she asked, her voice dropping, becoming the kind, loving Ceris that she usually was. How strange that people can change character so easily, become different types of personality. You think you know people, you think you know them so well, you think you've got them in the bag. But you never have really.

I smiled up at her. 'My head's fine.' And it was. I had no hangover at all, which made me even more suspicious about last night, even more convinced I'd been drugged or that something very peculiar indeed had happened. Perhaps Ceris was in on it? She was being too normal, too unaffected. I scratched my stomach. Ceris kissed me. I stared at her. She didn't look real, she was in on the act, perhaps *she* had drugged me. Ceris put her head on one side, then silently went to the shower. I stared out of the window whilst listening to the sound of the water rushing.

I shook my head as if to shake out the rubbish that was zooming around inside it. From time to time Ceris sighed. After a little more time she started to sing.

IX

The TV screen hissing like a spayed cat, representing nothingness by means of chaotic black and white dots. I realised what the noise was, got off the bed and stumbled through the vague darkness to the illuminated envelope of the screen. I looked at the little black and white dots, dancing round each other like bacteria on a slide; electrons in an atom. Random life, jumping around, furiously going about its business, arguing, jostling, speeding here and there, even though all the jostling and the arguing and the speeding is futile.

When the TV is showing nothing, why isn't it just still? Why isn't it silent? Why isn't it a peaceful, painless quiet blackness? It's always a buzzing, chaotic noise. Nature abhorring a vacuum, even in the tiny corner of a little Bruges hotel at two in the morning.

I looked around the room. It was bathed in blue light from the television. I looked back at the screen. The dots still danced with inexhaustible energy. I looked at them and frowned, begging them to slow down. They reminded me of a roomful of two year olds. The dots were black and white. Why was the room bathed in blue? I shook my head, felt around the unfamiliar controls of the TV, and eventually found the off button.

I fell back into bed, still seeing the fury of the TV screen and feeling exhausted. I was aware of nothing else until a shaft of light as solid as oak – a beam of light, I thought – fell slantwise across the bed. A naked Ceris, her body haloed and glowing gold, reached across and kissed me on the forehead.

X

Looking at the TV that morning, looking at Richard and Judy interviewing someone I'd never heard of who kept smiling knowingly at the camera, proud of how famous he was, I thought, yes, the television is just a box with electrical impulses running through it... it is entirely chaotic... there is no purpose to it, it has no thought of its own, it is just meaningless and unformed... how can Richard and Judy be on it anyway, I'm in Belgium... I got up and switched them off.

The long windows that reached to the floor stared at me expressionlessly, their vacant looks – glazed expressions – observing me blankly. I saw my reflection in them three times over and I thought, the panes of glass are looking at me. Staring at me. I could see through my reflections to the garden beyond, and I thought, the windows can see through me.

In the garden there was a stone statue, unusually horizontal, of a naked woman lying on her front. Although it was stone, there was a hole in the woman's back; the torso caved in, like a skull that had been smashed. The stone was bleached white and looked like bone.

The rain rolling down the window sounded like the hiss of void-ridden TV. Half the noise abruptly stopped, like the TV being turned off. Ceris emerged from the shower. I shook my head slightly, emerging from the distant place I'd been lost in. She walked up to me slowly, cautiously, and kissed me wetly. Her hair flicked round my face.

'All right?' she murmured.

I managed to smile. I felt absent, as if it was an effort to be there, as if I didn't quite know where I was. As if I needed food, or had had too much sleep.

'Fine,' I eventually said. I thought, I adore you.

She put the TV on, dropped her towel on the floor, and flopped onto the bed. She slithered about as she tried to find the remote control.

She stretched nakedly. Outside, the stone statue glanced in and watched Ceris from the corner of its eye. I drew the heavy curtains across the blank windows.

Outside, I stood under the statue of van Eyck and pulled my coat around me. The movement didn't make me any warmer, it just trapped cold air. Some leaves fell about me during a sudden gust of wind. The sound was exactly like that of bubble wrap being gently rubbed.

When I stood on the leaves they crunched as if made of ice. I looked up at the statue. It was the green of mint ice cream. When I reached up and touched it, it was cold and metallic like mint ice cream too. I resisted the temptation to lick it. More leaves fell. The sky was a fierce bright pale blue, like swimming pool tiles, and was painful on my eyes as I looked up at it. The statue moved about slightly and a black wiggly line formed around it as I tried to look at the sky whilst keeping my eyes fully open.

I looked up at the houses, the strange, two-dimensional crenellated fronts stuck in front of the normal sloping roofs as if designed by a child. If I pushed them hard enough, they would topple over. I looked along the street and it seemed to be made of cardboard; a kit that someone had put together. One good shove would bring it all down. What would be behind it all? Something that I couldn't even begin to conceive of.

Or there would be nothing? Not even blackness, just – nothing. When you reach the edge of the universe, what's on the other side?

I looked towards the canal. It didn't flow, it just sat there, as if it were a representation of a canal; brown model-maker's putty, presenting a very good impression of a canal but you know it's not real. The way you notice a special effect in a film and you're impressed by how good it is; but you still know it's just an effect, because you've noticed it.

I looked up at van Eyck and he made me think of the *Arnolfini Portrait*, which made me think of the girl the other night, which made me think of her green eyes, which made me think of the statue outside the cathedral, which made me think of the pale greenness of van Eyck. My glasses started to frost over. I shivered, wondered why I was standing out here in the freezing cold. I wrapped my coat around me and walked along the canal back to the hotel.

XI

A passing girl offered us champagne. Ceris took some, nodding up at her. I watched Belgium turn into France. There was no announcement or sign. It just happened gradually and invisibly, like a tadpole becoming a frog. Ceris swilled the champagne in the round, almost globular little glass.

'I was thinking when we were in Bruges,' she said.

'Yes?'

'I was going to leave you.'

The train stopped, the countryside froze, the people in the seats behind stopped moving. The film ran out and the plastic frames flapped on the projector as it turned blindly round and round. She looked at me, the line of her mouth firm, the eyes unyielding. She wasn't going to continue until I said something.

'Oh,' I said.

'You're never happy. I don't make you happy. That was why I was going to leave you.'

I struggled to say something. 'You do make me happy,' I managed eventually.

'You lie awake at nights, when you think I'm asleep, and you stare into space. And I hear you sighing. And that sighing sounds like the cosmos, weary because it's got to carry on existing, immensely, forever.'

I looked around to see if there were any roaming girls so that I could change my mind about not having champagne.

'So I thought, this is pointless, I've had enough of this, it's not going anywhere.'

Slowly, outside, the countryside started to move again. The hum of the carriage switched back on again.

'You use the past tense,' I said. 'Does this mean you're *not* going to leave me?'

She drained the wine and set the glass down on the little table with a decisive movement of her hand. 'Yes,' she said, 'I don't want to leave you.' She frowned, as if disagreeing with her own thoughts.

'What made you change your mind?' My voice sounded unnaturally calm inside my own head, but my heart thumped like a caged animal.

She shrugged. Perhaps it was best that she didn't say anything. She looked out of the window for a moment, then back at me, in fact slightly past me, her lips moving almost imperceptibly. I knew her well enough to know that she was going to change the subject, and was curious to know what it would be.

'Weren't that couple strange?' she produced from somewhere.

I paused before answering. 'Which couple?'

'Oh, you know. The two who were there the night you got really drunk. That odd chap and that girl who thought she was famous.'

I looked at her. Had Irena really kissed me, had I imagined it, had I dreamt it? Had I gone to bed with her? Was I drugged and hallucinating; was I drunk and had fantasised it; perhaps it had really happened? Perhaps Ceris knew all about it and was testing me now? After all, where had she gone? I had followed her out of the bar and she had disappeared. Or had she? If I'd imagined it, she could have been there all the time. Perhaps she knew and didn't mind and thought I couldn't remember? Should I ask her? She studied me impassively, her jawline straight, not giving anything away. Should I say anything?

'Yes,' I said. It all seemed so long ago now, so far away. 'Yes, they were odd. She seemed so affected. I thought – ha – famous – as if! She probably sings with some band who perform in bars.'

Ceris raised her eyebrows in agreement.

'I mean,' I continued, 'everyone reckons they're famous these days, don't they? Everyone's got a recording contract or is going to be starring on TV or is writing a book. She's no more famous than you or me.' I knew now that I had not gone to bed with her.

It had all been a fiction, it had all been made up. The whole evening was unreal, a façade – the room, the famous girl, the idea of sleeping with her.

The edge of Ceris's mouth turned up. 'Yes... sad in a way. He seemed... proud of her.' She looked around as she searched for the word, and 'proud' was not right, but she said it anyway and moved on. 'You could tell she didn't really have what it takes to be really good.'

'How do you mean?'

'You could just tell.'

The train trundled on rhythmically. Did she know? Was there anything to know? If I said something it might give it all away. But if there was nothing to give away, did it matter? But otherwise I'd never know whether she knew. *Was* there anything to give away? Did that matter anyway, now we were going home? Had anything happened? Did it mean anything if it had, if I couldn't remember and Ceris wasn't saying anything? What did it mean? I was brought back to my seat by her voice, but I didn't hear what she said.

'Sorry?'

She smiled at me. 'I said, "I love you." '

XII

I looked out of the window and thought, what's the point of it all, it's all random, it's all meaningless, perhaps she should have left me after all. Perhaps I should leave her. I glanced at her; she was brushing lunch's crumbs from her lap and carefully, slightly drunkenly, pouring water into her wine glass. I could never leave you, I thought.

She looked up at me and feigned a frown. 'What are you smiling at?'

'Nothing,' I said.

I stared at the glass of water and watched little bubbles form on the surface. Even a glass of water cannot stay still. The train bumped over a track and the water swished from side to side.

I must have fallen asleep because when I woke up it was dark. Nodding into consciousness I thought, I can't possibly have been asleep so long that it's got dark. I frowned. Ceris noticed the frown, and its reason. 'We're in the tunnel,' she said.

'Ah.'

'Go back to sleep if you want to.'

I looked at her glass of water. When I looked more closely I realised that it wasn't water any more, but had miraculously become wine. The girl with the trolley must have been along. I realised Ceris was watching me. Self-consciously, I put my hands uncertainly on the table, then on my lap, then by my sides, so that one hand hung over the edge of the seat and the other hand rested on the seat. I tried to make the hands look nonchalant. The hand on the seat came into contact with the free Eurostar magazine; I picked it up and flicked through it.

'I think I'll have a doze,' said Ceris. She leant forward, kissed me and settled back in her seat.

On page 14, highlights of the week in Brussels. A half-page picture of a girl, strikingly beautiful. My skin prickled as I looked at the picture, but I couldn't work out why. I read the text. 'Irena Marsalis, darling of the Dutch, plays in Brussels this week to what will no doubt will be a packed, ten-thousand-strong hall. Book your seats now to see the singer renowned on the Continent as the greatest exponent of...'

So she was famous after all. I dropped the magazine on the

seat and looked outside at the apparently motionless blackness.

We shot into light. My ears popped. I took my glasses off and cleaned them on my jumper. The world fudged and smeared for a moment and when I put my glasses back on I saw Ceris looking out of the window. After a moment or two, the newly appeared England lost its novelty. She put her seat back and closed her eyes. I stared at her. I kept staring at her. She absently, slowly, pushed her hair behind her ear and breathed deeply. I stared at her some more.

translations

*you cannot always be drawing because half your life
you are asleep or eating or making love*
sven berlin

it has taken me my whole life to learn how not to draw
matisse

I

The fireplace was a fake, but Luisa and Jay were proud of it. It was made of blackish metal and was complemented by a purple rug that stretched away from it like a napkin tied round its neck. One of Luisa's early pictures hung on the wall above it. On the opposite wall, the one that in most houses stays blank because no-one knows what to put on it, was a kind of fisherman's net with Christmas lights embedded in it. The Victorian floorboards had been put in by Jay the week before. There was an archway too.

Luisa was the first of Sally's friends to move into her own house. Sally and Robert were visiting for the first time; to Sally it was like being seventeen again and visiting relations. There was a strong smell of newly cut flowers and coffee. Luisa ran her hands through her hair, tucked her shirt into her jeans and examined her fingers, which were orange. 'Coffee?' she asked.

'That would be lovely,' said Sally automatically. She had brought a bottle of wine and felt like opening it, but perhaps that wasn't the way Luisa did things, now that she had become sophisticated. Sally looked round and tried to think of something intelligent to say. 'I like your fisherman's net thing,' she said.

'Thanks. It came from Habitat.'

Sally nodded. 'Was it terribly expensive?' she asked, pulling the side of her mouth down in an oral shrug.

'Oh, I don't know, Jay bought it. He's on the mailing list,' she added. Sally raised her eyebrows in appreciation. '*Right*,' she said knowingly.

They sat down on the beanbags and listened to the scratching of the chinchilla in its cage. Sally found herself sinking back in her beanbag. Luisa had perfect control of how she sat, and perched elegantly. Sally found herself descending until she was parallel with Luisa's feet. Luisa had silver toenail polish and the soles of her feet were black.

Sally decided that the pause provided a good opportunity to hand her present over. Luisa's eyes lit up and she unwrapped it enthusiastically. It was an early edition of *Dream Story*. Luisa was thoroughly impressed. It was probably very valuable.

'I was going to get you the *Eyes Wide Shut* video,' Sally was saying nervously, not sure what the look in Luisa's eyes commu-

Conversations with Magic Stones

nicated, 'but I couldn't find it.' Now that Luisa was so cosmopolitan, would she like it? Sally chewed the inside of her mouth.

'No, no.' Luisa ran her hands over the covers of the book. She opened it up and peeked inside to see if anyone had written their name or damaged it in any other way. 'No,' she said, 'I'd rather have the book. I haven't read it since, oh... years ago. It's not a first edition, is it?'

'No, I don't think so.' Sally looked at her uncertainly, then glanced at Robert to see why he was so silent. Robert was looking up at the fisherman's net in fascination. Eventually he turned to Luisa. 'If one of the bulbs blows,' he said, 'do they all go?'

Luisa shrugged skittishly and dropped the book on the glass coffee table. 'I've no idea,' she said, lifting her palms outwards in unconcerned abandon.

'The film is so different, isn't it,' she said, drawing Luisa's attention back to the book, 'and Tom and Nicole are nothing like Fridolin and Albertine, are they, but the scenes themselves have been lifted almost you know, what's the word, verbatim, from the book, you know, and dropped into contemporary New York. I've never seen an adaptation of a book that uses the text as a, what's the word, *template* in the way *Eyes Wide Shut* does, have you?'

Robert was looking out of the window. A burnt-out car was mounted on the pavement, apparently competing for the Turner Prize. The tyres were flat and had melted into the tarmac, making it look like a sculpture on a stand. A man walked past, his stooped body led by a cigarette, which puffed as it pulled him along.

Sally shook her head imperceptibly as she looked at Robert. Why couldn't he join in, he could at least join in, he wasn't stupid, or perhaps she was just assuming he wasn't stupid, perhaps he was stupid.

'Which road is this?' Robert asked, his voice billowing out loudly in the vacuum that had developed between them. Luisa shrugged dismissively, as if the road she lived on was another issue that Jay looked after. Sally shrugged too, in an attempt to ally herself with Luisa. Sally didn't have a clue what part of London they were in, let alone which road. Robert had had to visit three petrol stations to get this far, and Sally didn't want any further information to complicate things. There was a pause.

'Except that Kubrick was such a fraud, wasn't he?' said Luisa.

Robert tried to stand up as he wanted to go the toilet, but found getting up out of the beanbag an undignified and noisy activity, and when he noticed Sally and Luisa watching him, cut his losses and stayed where he was. He could always go to the toilet later. He sat quietly, careful not to disturb any of the beans in the bag. He looked out of the window again for a bit, but it wasn't very interesting so he searched for an alternative and finally looked idly towards the archway. Jay was standing in it, staring down at them. Robert jumped. The beans squidged noisily. Sally and Luisa glanced at Robert, then followed his gaze up towards Jay.

Jay wore pale blue jeans and a black shirt and had bare feet. Luisa shuffled round on her beanbag and smiled up at him. 'This is Jay,' she said, as if it might have been the postman. Jay nodded, but was otherwise motionless. There was a bit of a pause, not as long as the last one.

'What do you mean, he was a fraud?' asked Sally.

'Well, you know,' said Luisa, emerging effortlessly from her beanbag and floating towards the kitchen. 'Pretending he was a great director, and that everything he did was very intellectual and that it was so complex that it appeared not to make sense. Whereas really he just wanted to make thrillers, but he wasn't very good at them. That's why they didn't make sense.'

Conversations with Magic Stones

She disappeared through the archway. Jay stood with his arms folded, leaning against the door, not responding to Sally's nervous smile. Sally pulled a curl of hair forward and chewed at it uncertainly. Robert's beanbag made moaning noises, as if it wanted to be let out. Robert knew how it felt. Sally glared at him. Robert, mortified, kept his bottom still.

Luisa came back with coffee. Steam wafted and Luisa's face disappeared behind it.

'Er – ' said Robert.

'Haven't we got anything to drink?' Jay interrupted, and disappeared back through the archway.

When Luisa was back from the kitchen and Jay was installed behind a bottle of wine, Sally nudged Robert and with a murmured 'oh yes, of course,' he handed his presents over to Luisa. She unwrapped them and squealed. 'Oh they're lovely,' she said. 'I love Chinese stuff.' She looked more closely. 'Japanese stuff,' she corrected. Robert was pleased.

'I don't know how old they are,' he said. 'One of them is slightly cracked on the rim,' he added apologetically.

'Oh, I think that adds to it,' said Luisa, her eyes moving from one pot to the other. Robert was pleased again. 'I love these gold bits.'

Robert wiped his hands against each other. They felt clammy and uncomfortable. He looked at the pots through new eyes, now that he had handed them over. They were pretty, but looked small and insignificant in Luisa's hands. In the antique shop he had fallen in love with them, they were beautiful; but now they looked dirty and cracked and cheap. He had paid forty pounds for them (having haggled from forty-five). Now they looked like seven or eight quid's worth and let's face it that isn't really much to spend on a friend you've known since school. Sally's *Dream Story* sat squarely and insultingly on the table in front of him, large and solid and proud, the page edgings glinting at him like a man with gold teeth. You know where you are with a book, Robert thought sadly.

'I think they're about a hundred years old,' he said into the silence.

'Right.' Luisa had turned one of the pots upside down and was reading the bottom. Robert's head fell and he stared at his crotch regretfully.

Luisa brought her assessment to a close. 'I love them,' she concluded. She stepped over to Robert and hugged him. He smelt her perfume. It was the same perfume she used to wear at school. Random images appeared in his brain all at once, fighting each other for supremacy. The short hair she had had then; the evening they all went to the cinema and he was sick on the way home; the picture she drew of him on the playing field; the way she used to wrinkle her nose up – she doesn't do that any more –

Luisa took the pots over to the fake fireplace. She rearranged a few things on the mantelpiece and put the pots either side of her headless Greek figures.

'So what do you think of my flat?' she asked, turning back to them.

'Oh, it's lovely,' said Sally automatically.

Jay stood beside Luisa like her shadow. 'We saw lots of places for the same money before this one,' she said, 'and they were just awful. We held out and I'm really glad we did because we love it here.' She sat down and flicked her hair behind her ear and looked at Sally's book. Robert leaned back on the sofa and sipped his tea, keeping the mug in front of his face.

Conversations with Magic Stones

Alison arrived. She gave Luisa a purple globular lamp. 'It looks a bit like a sea anemone,' she explained. They all nodded. They all thought, we can see without being told that it looks like a sea anemone.

Alison squeezed it. It compressed wherever you pressed a finger into it, and then sprang back into shape. 'It's wonderful,' said Luisa. 'I love it.' She kissed Alison.

'It's lovely,' added Sally.

Robert looked at his pots on the mantelpiece. They were growing on him again. He turned his head from side to side to look at them. They looked distinguished and old and of a different class than purple lamps that looked like sea anemones.

Jay opened a second bottle of wine. Robert and Sally had given up on the beanbags and had graduated to the leather sofa. Let the others sit on the beanbags, Robert thought boldly. Luisa came over to the sofa and squeezed herself between Sally and Robert. She put her arms round Robert.

'So,' she said, 'how come you never visit me?'

'Well,' he said. 'You know.'

Two new people stood at the door. Luisa jumped up. 'This is Kif and this is Jenna,' she announced. Jenna, spiky red hair, 70s patterned jumper and brown leather jacket, looked round. 'Wow,' she said, seeing the purple lamp, 'what a fantastic lamp!' She touched it. 'Oh, it squeezes when you touch it!' She played with it for a bit.

'It's a sea anemone,' said Sally. Jenna frowned and looked at her. 'Really?' She sat down. Robert wondered if she would notice his pots.

Kif nodded at people he knew, dropped onto a beanbag and started rolling a joint.

Sally jumped up at nine o'clock and said she had to go. 'I've got an early shift tomorrow,' she explained. 'I'm not boring,' she added, for the benefit of Jenna and Kif, who nodded slowly at her through a cloud of smoke. They were sprawled across the beanbags, had put dark glasses on and their mouths hung open as the smoke rose slowly above them. Robert was reminded of footage of nuclear test sites.

Sally got her coat then looked around the entire flat for her car keys. After a while Luisa and Alison joined in the hunt. Kif watched the bustling activity with great interest and eventually the car keys were located underneath his left buttock. 'How did they get there?' he asked, genuinely surprised.

'Can I come with you?' Robert asked Sally timidly.

'Yes of course you can,' she said, 'I might get lost otherwise.' They got up to go. Luisa barred the way. 'Where do you think you're going?' she demanded, pretending to be cross.

'I've got an early tomorrow,' Sally said apologetically.

'You haven't got an early, though, have you? Unless you've also become a nurse?' She raised an eyebrow questioningly at him.

Robert shook his head. 'No,' he admitted, 'I haven't.'

'That's settled then. You can sleep on the sofa bed.'

'I really don't – '

Sally and Luisa were kissing each other loudly. 'Yes I *know*,' Luisa was shrieking, 'yes we *must!*' Robert went back into the living room and sat on the window sill.

Luisa thanked Sally for the book and bustled her out of the door. 'See you next week,' she said, closing the door behind her. Robert sat by the window, wondering why there were no curtains. Something to do with Luisa being an artist, he imagined.

He watched Sally outside, looking up and down the street with her finger on her lips, trying to remember which way the car was. She faded into a smudge behind Robert's breath on the glass.

Harry and Jo arrived. They looked reasonably normal so Robert walked over and sat next to them, and was about to introduce himself when they started kissing passionately.

Robert looked round the room. Luisa was showing Jenna a colour chart and Jenna was comparing various shades of green against her skin. Robert drank a glass of wine in one mouthful and wondered whether to risk a trip out to the kitchen in search of the bottle. Alison got up, found a Chemical Brothers CD and put it on extremely loudly. Kif was almost shaken off his beanbag. He looked underneath him, wondering vaguely why the ground was moving.

Robert looked at the gradually thickening haze of brownish smoke that was enveloping the room and wondered where the sofa bed would be installed. He tried to open the window, but it wouldn't budge. He looked down the street again, hoping to see Sally walking back up it. He busied himself looking at a cat sitting idly on a wall beyond the burnt-out car. The cat yawned and settled itself down for a nap. A child threw a stone at it from an upstairs window.

Jay stood framed in the doorway. He seemed to be looking at Robert; and Robert, all attempts at masking his unhappiness abandoned, watched him like a lost puppy.

'Come over here,' Jay said across the room. Robert looked up as if wondering who he was talking to, then walked over.

'Look at this,' Jay said, nodding his head towards the bedroom. 'Something to show you.'

Robert meekly followed him. A large double bed with black

sheets dominated the room. No other furniture. The walls were white. Hanging above the bed was a large canvas. Jay nodded towards it. 'That's what Luisa gave me for Christmas,' he said.

There was a large patch of red, roughly painted, and a darker slab of red below it. A vague purplish line separated the two colours. The edges of the canvas were unpainted.

Silence fell between them like a curtain.

'What do you think?' Jay prompted.

Robert tried to think of something intelligent to say. 'It's like Rothko,' he came out with eventually.

Jay frowned. 'Well, no, it's nothing like Rothko. Well,' he qualified, 'of course it is, it's exactly like Rothko, on the *surface*.'

Knowing that he wouldn't win whatever he said, Robert decided to say what he liked. 'You see, for me it's just a daub. It doesn't do anything for me.'

Robert shrugged. He felt the great manacles of trying to be sociable fall effortlessly from his shoulders and thud resoundingly on the floor.

'Right,' said Jay.

'I mean it's probably because I'm not an artist,' Robert acknowledged.

'No, it's difficult, isn't it, it's all *perception*.'

'Luisa used to do much more representational stuff,' Robert said apologetically. The manacles were re-attaching themselves to his ankles. He tried to smile.

Jay nodded. 'The problem is,' he said slowly, 'that in the end, representation doesn't say anything new. Non-representation has a problem because it can be misinterpreted as not saying anything at all. Why does a painting have to say anything anyway? A piece of music doesn't say anything. It's what it makes you feel.'

'Well, no, no, yes, quite.' Pause. Okay. Robert was getting the hang of this conversation. 'This doesn't make me feel anything,' he said.

Jay nodded, and looked at him carefully, and nodded again. 'That's a shame. I think it's very successful. It achieves what it set out to do. That's all any of us can hope for, isn't it?'

Jenna sat rolling a joint. 'The problem with trying to live in an anarchy,' she was saying to Luisa, 'is that other people don't abide by the rules. I mean, I live in a house on my own, and I keep the garden nice and tidy. I grow vegetables. And the people next door, their garden's a total mess. But because they own their house and I'm squatting, they want to get me thrown out.' She took a long drag and as she breathed out she shook her head, so the smoke wafted back and forth. 'Doesn't make sense, does it?'

II

Most people had gone and the music had been switched off. Jenna was discussing the crimes of supermarkets with Jay, who clutched a bottle of wine to his chest like a suckling baby. Their voices sounded loud and resonant in the loud, vibrating silence.

'Fair trade, for instance. What a joke that is. They make the teabags a bit more expensive, so that the people who pick the tea get paid a bit more. And we all think, wow, the supermarkets are so ethical and wonderful. But it's the customers who pay the extra few pennies so that the workers get paid more.'

'Well – that's good isn't it?' Jay looked at her a bit foggily. 'A fair price for a fair – ' he jumped slightly in his seat as he hiccupped – 'product.'

Jenna smiled at him as at an innocent child. 'Who was it who forced the tea pickers to cut their prices to below subsistence levels in the first place?' she asked. 'The supermarkets, so they could make their obscene profits. They *caused* the poverty, because they had such clout, they're such large buyers that they can demand what they like. So with 'fair trade', *we* pay for the workers to get paid properly. And the supermarkets still make the inflated profit, and at the same time, get loads of credit for being ethical!' She blew an exclamation mark of smoke at Jay.

Jay nodded in agreement through all this, and continued nodding after she had stopped talking.

Robert felt the evening slowly unwinding like a spring. He sat on a beanbag, feeling the room floating up and down and trying to keep his feet on the floor. Luisa knelt beside him, her head resting on his knee. She looked up at him. 'So why don't you go out with Sally?'

'Well. You know.'

She shrugged. 'I think you should. She'd be good for you.'

'She's a bit silly.'

Luisa thumped him on the arm. 'That's one of the reasons she'd be good for you.'

Robert smiled at her. 'Why didn't you let her take me home then?' he asked. Luisa opened her eyes wide and shrieked like a seabird. 'Because I haven't seen you for a *year*,' she said, 'a *year*, and I wasn't going to let you get away with leaving so early, that's why! Will you be okay on the sofa bed?' she added, her voice dropping about two octaves.

Jenna sat cross-legged on the sofa, rolling another joint. Jay crawled across the floor to Robert. 'I hope you'll be all right,' he said sincerely.

'Oh, I'll be fine. Fine.'

'I'm very drunk,' Jay said confidentially, looking behind him in case anyone might hear this confession, 'so Luisa and I are going to bed. Is there anything you want?'

'No, no, really. You go to bed.'

Jay looked at him and nodded. 'Is everything... is everything all right?' You don't... you don't... mind?' he said, waving an arm around to encompass the room, the smoke, Jenna, the villages of overflowing ashtrays.

'No, I don't mind.'

'Good, good. Um, Jenna's staying too.'

'Ah.'

'She's quite content curling up on the sofa, she does it all the time.'

'Right.'

'I think she prefers it here. Her neighbours complain when she comes in late. You don't mind, do you?'

'No.'

He crawled out through the archway. The silence stung Robert's ears. He started to untie the sofabed, which Luisa had left by the window for him, then looked down at the bottles and the remains of pizza, beer cans and cigarette ends that lay at his feet. Robert went to the toilet to look at himself in the mirror and wonder why he ever came. He usually found that this calmed him down.

Lazily above Jenna's head hung a pall of smoke. 'Hi,' she said when Robert came back. He nodded at her.

'We haven't really talked, have we? I'm Jenna.'

'Hello.'

Robert pulled his shirt and trousers off, and let the cube of sofabed unwrap and fall where it wanted, on top of the bottles and pizza and everything else. He lay on top of it and turned his head away from Jenna.

'Do you want some of this? It might relax you.'

'No.'

'She's lovely, Luisa, isn't she?'

Robert closed his eyes. 'I don't walk to tank about sumpermarteks,' he muttered, and was asleep instantly.

Robert dreamed that he was at an underwear party that Sally had organised. Sally was in a transparent bra and knickers. Luisa wore plain black underwear with stockings and suspenders, and Jenna was in a see-through body. Robert came to the party wearing a coat and was unhappy about being there. Luisa and Jenna cajoled him, telling him it was an underwear party, for goodness sake, and making him take his coat off. He rather uncertainly emerged in his pink lace bra and g-string. They regarded it as completely normal. He chatted with Sally and Alison, who wore a silky red top and French knickers, about what books they'd read lately.

Outside Robert's mind, the sun rose on the abandoned vehicles and Jenna uncoiled from the sofa and coughed.

III

The kitchen was bleached white with light. The sun hung in slabs in the living room because of the curtainless windows. The cloud of smoke from last night was still visible. As Robert woke up in the same position he had fallen asleep in, he was surprised to discover that he did not have a headache. He pulled his trousers on, but couldn't find his socks or shirt. The room was empty. He sat staring into space, unable to think of anything.

Cans, bottles and pizza had been cleaned away, the tables and chairs were restored to their former positions and the books were neatly back on their shelves from where they had been scattered. The purple lamp glowed in the strong sunlight. Robert noticed that the sofa bed must have been pulled up with him still asleep on it, because when he folded it up, there was no rubbish underneath.

He wandered through the archway, found a teabag and was looking for a kettle when he noticed Luisa and Jenna sitting on the balcony.

'Hello.'

Robert shielded his eyes against the light.

'Did you sleep okay?'

'Er – yes.'

'Do you want a cup of tea?' Luisa asked, looking at the teabag he was still gripping.

'Yes. I can't find the kettle.'

Luisa swung her bare feet in through the window and jumped in. Her shirt rode up as she slid over the sill, and he saw the blue jewel in her belly button. She stood pulling her shirt down. 'That's the kettle,' she said, pointing at a transparent sphere half filled with water.

'Oh. I thought it was a goldfish bowl.' Robert felt his mouth seizing up. Just stay calm and stop talking, he told himself.

'It's great, isn't it?'

Jenna jumped in. 'It's a beautiful day out there,' she said. 'I thought I might take my top off.' The kettle started boiling. Robert dropped his teabag.

Jenna's expression changed and she grabbed Robert's arm. 'Have you seen in here?' she asked, tugging him into the bedroom. 'Yes, I – ' he began, but Jenna interrupted. 'It's *fantastic*.'

Robert looked up. He saw the painting that he had hated last night. Shafts of light came in through the skylight and the open window. The painting shone. The reds played and danced. Robert breathed in the spring air. 'Isn't it *beautiful?*' said Jenna, her mouth open in admiration. Her teeth glowed white. Robert looked back at the painting. The messy brushwork, which last night had seemed dull and amateurish, now writhed and wriggled as if trying to leap off the canvas. The two panels of colour fought each other for supremacy. Parts of the painting were deeper than others, there was real energy and lyricism. It was wonderful.

'Isn't it just the greatest picture you've ever seen?' said Jenna. 'Luisa painted it for Jay for Christmas.'

Robert nodded in silence. The the oil fought against the canvas, the colours were rich and vibrant. Robert found himself salivating. It made him hungry. He heard Jenna next to him, her breathing loud and ecstatic. Around them, the room was white and hot and brilliant

IV

The Holloway Road gleamed. There had been a shower of rain and the strong sunlight made the tarmac glisten like a night sky.

'This is it,' said Luisa. 'The Workers' Caff.'

'Fantastic.'

'You can get an enormous breakfast for four quid, toast and cup of tea all in,' Luisa advised. 'I particularly recommend the fried eggs – exquisite.'

Jenna went up to the counter to order. Robert sat in a red spongy seat with the foam coming out of it on all sides, like a bursting sausage. He looked round. A man with a bright red face ate chips. Two Swedish girls who had heavily lacquered hair and faces ate toast. They wore white PVC zip-up jackets. As they ate, little cracks appeared in the make-up wherever their faces moved.

Jenna came back. 'Three full breakfasts coming up, and one vegetarian combo for me.' She sat next to Robert.
Jay groaned.
'What?' asked Luisa, holding his leg.
'Perhaps I should have just ordered a boiled egg.'
'Are you still feeling ill?' Luisa stroked his hair, then dropped her hand into his lap and rubbed his arm. 'I'll go and get you some water.'
'Thank you.' He bent down like an elderly man and kissed her hand.

The breakfasts arrived. They were unashamedly huge. Two sausages, four rashers of bacon, two fried eggs, a garden of mushrooms, a grilled tomato and a lake of baked beans oozing over the edge of the plate.
'Isn't it *fabulous*?' said Luisa. 'This is just the best place on the planet. Jay and I always come here after a heavy night, don't we Jay?'
Jay stared at his breakfast.
'There's so much snobbery about food,' Luisa continued. 'I mean the whole point about food is that it fills you up, it gives you energy, and you can spend what you have and you can enjoy it. And that's exactly what you get here. Look at the different types of people you get in here. I always want to start painting them.'
Next to them, an elderly woman in a neck scarf sat with a small yappy dog perched on the seat beside her. She was intent-

ly reading an article in the *Daily Express* about Hitler's jaw, which was being displayed in a museum in Moscow. It would have been shown years ago, but had just been put on display now because it had finally been proven as genuine.

What does it matter whether it's genuine or not? thought Robert. It's just a bit of skull. But because it's Hitler's, people are going to pay money and queue up and look at it. If it had been proved not to have been Hitler's, no one would be interested. And the actual object is identical now to how it was before it had been proved genuine; there isn't anything intrinsically different about what you're going to look at. But somehow it has become completely different. It has meaning.

From time to time, the woman put a bit of sausage on her fork and fed it to the dog. The dog ate it uncertainly, looking down at the ground and moving its head up and down rhythmically as it chewed. It swallowed, looked slightly surprised, then lifted its head up towards the old woman, waiting for the next mouthful.

'I love this place. What you see is what you get. It's the most genuine place I know. It's so real.'

Outside, a blue Ford Escort drove slowly past. A hammer and sickle flag waved from the window, there were loudspeakers on the roof and on its side 'Vote Communist' was painted in large red letters. The two Swedish girls got up, left money on the table and walked out.

Jay watched them go. 'I don't feel very well,' he murmured.

In a second-hand bookshop a recovering Jay got very excited by a book he found by somebody called Cabr Volsung.

'Look at this,' he said. 'Have you heard of it?'

Robert shook his head.

Conversations with Magic Stones

'It's an account of life under the Khmer Rouge, and when it was published it got acclaimed as being so real and insightful, and this chap was showered with awards for all the hell he went through and being so brave to keep a diary. And then guess what?'

'?'

'It turned out he'd made it all up. It was complete fabrication. So the book has totally disappeared, and I've always wanted to read it but you can't get hold of it now.

'Look at the names on the back...' Robert's eye trailed down the list of well-known journalists and writers, all heaping praise on the book.

'Amazing isn't it? All taken in, and all saying how marvellously accurate and harrowing it is. What a fraud.'

Robert found a paperback copy of *Dream Story* for 50p. On the way out, Jay grabbed his arm. Robert looked up at him questioningly.

'You didn't like me to begin with did you?' said Robert in an undertone.

'No.'

'But you like me now.'

'Yes.'

The girls waited impatiently outside. 'Everyone goes to Hyde Park,' Luisa was saying as Robert and Jay emerged. 'We'll go to Regent's Park.'

'I've never been to Regent's Park,' Jenna said.

They walked four abreast alongside the Georgian houses that curved like a sponge cake on the approach to the park. The yellowish stucco was like marzipan; Robert felt an urge to break a bit off and taste it. 'There's the Prince's Trust,' said Luisa. 'What a brilliant idea. You go in and tell Prince Charles you need some money and he gives it to you.'

'Does he really?' said Jenna. Luisa nodded. 'Fantastic,' said Jenna.

They walked through the park. London Zoo rose in the distance like a Moroccan castle.

'I want to go and explore,' said Jay, jumping up and down. 'Take me to the zoo, Luisa, take me to the zoo.'

'You'll have to forgive my boyfriend. He's terribly puerile.'

'I was puerile, until you took my purity from me, you beast.'

'We're not going to the zoo, we're going to take a boat out.'

They walked along the winding paths that led to the lake. Luisa and Jay walked hand in hand. Jenna squealed when she walked in the grass and mud squelched through her sandals. No one seemed sure where the lake was, but they all seemed confident that they would find it eventually. Jenna took her sandals off.

It was a lazy afternoon, a moment in time that would stay preserved and not disappear, and they would all remember that precise moment as clearly as if they had a photograph of it.

'I was thinking about that book, Jay. Him being a fraud, and being condemned for it.' Robert walked along with his hands in his pockets, looking at the ground.

'Yes?'

'You could just say he's written a great novel. So great that everyone who read it thought it was real. What he did was only terrible because he claimed it was true. It could still be a great work – doesn't matter whether it happened or not.'

'Yes. Perhaps he always intended to write a novel, then decided to publish it as a memoir to see if it would work. To see how real it was. If it was a really convincing novel, people would really believe it. And if people couldn't believe it, then it wasn't any good. Kosinski used to do that sort of thing. He – '

But they had reached the lake, and Luisa organised everyone. 'Let's get two boats.'

'We could all go in the same boat, couldn't we?' Robert asked anxiously, spotting immediately that Luisa's plan would leave him with Jenna.

'Oh but look,' said Luisa, pointing at the sign. 'The cost is per person, not per boat. So we may as well take two.'

'Ah. Right.' Robert nodded dubiously. He wasn't sure he could cope with being on his own with Jenna. It did not occur to him that Luisa had deliberately arranged it that way.

They bought their tickets from a friendly girl in a green hut who smiled broadly at each of them in turn. Robert followed Jenna.

Two men who spoke no English showed them to the boats and they clambered aboard. Jenna went first and sat in the rowing seat. A man with a moustache gave her the oars and babbled incomprehensibly. She nodded at him.

V

'Tell me when you get tired,' he said.

'Oh, I'm all right. I like rowing.'

She headed the boat out into the centre of the lake, a little behind Luisa and Jay. 'Shall we have a race?' Robert called over to them.

'No!' said Jenna in alarm. She grinned at him. Suddenly he seemed transformed. She had not expected him to say that, it was not the sort of thing she would have thought he would come out with. He was surprised too. He would not have thought he would have said it either.

Faces blurred as they passed on the bank. There were hundreds of people. It had become the first really warm weekend of the year. Gravitating towards the lake's edge like hippos, they came to rest on the gentle slopes and lay with limbs spread, staring up into the wide empty sky.

Robert glanced over at Jenna and saw she was looking at him.

'You seem very relaxed,' she said.

'Yes.'

'You're a bit quiet, aren't you? You're a quiet one.'

'Well...' he said, then stopped. There was a long pause.

'What do you do? For a living?'

He trailed a hand through the water. It made him feel thirsty.

'I'm a translator,' he said.

'Really?'

She seemed genuinely interested. He responded to this. 'Mmm. I get given books in Russian and I translate them into English.'

'Wow. *Really*? That's amazing.'

He shrugged. It never seemed amazing to him. 'I can do French as well, but everyone can do French. Russian's where I can make a living. Just. It's well paid, but I don't get enough hours a week to be comfortable.'

'It must be incredibly difficult.'

Robert looked across at Luisa and Jay. They were speeding away into the centre of the lake. A swan attempted to keep up alongside them.

'It is, but not for the reasons people think it is. It's easy to think of a suitable word or phrase and translate it. No problem there. It's the, what's the word, the opacity of the language that's the difficulty.'

'What's that supposed to mean?'

'Well. A phrase in Russian can have several different meanings.' Circles formed underneath the boat and spread out as Jenna steered the boat after Luisa and Jay.

'From the context,' Robert continued, 'you know what the main meaning is. But the writer knows that the other meanings exist, so writes very carefully in order to give a main meaning and several other, resonating meanings. Makes the complete text so much more satisfying.'

'Right.' Jenna's face reddened as she rowed.

'So when you're translating it, you're never going to have an entirely satisfactory result, because the resonances in Russian don't exist in the English equivalents of the phrase. You can get one or two of the meanings, but not all of them. A lot of the original will inevitably get lost.'

'Really?'

'Lots of them exploit this quality of Russian to great effect. Dostoyevsky; Chekhov particularly.'

A pause. The light rippled on the water. A sound like paper crumpling. Jenna steered the boat back towards the bank.

'Sometimes the text is like looking in a cracked mirror and seeing a hundred different reflections. All slightly different, but all essentially true.'

Jenna looked at Robert. The water reflected on her face. 'So you have to pick what seems the best one and stick with that?'

'Yes. I'm doing them all a disservice really.'

'But even more of a disservice if you didn't translate it at all.'

He nodded. Jenna put her head on one side. Her eyes were green from the sunlight on the water. The boat floated under an overhanging tree.

Robert looked at a house that looked like a chateau. An odd

kind of duck with an orange head swam in front of them. Jenna watched it. 'What's that called?'

'I don't know.'

She rowed more slowly.

'Do you want me to take over?' he asked.

'No, no, I'm fine.' Robert listened to the sound of her breathing, the ducks rippling the water, the smell of flowers as they neared the bank, the smell of the bark from the trees.

'I work in an antiques shop,' Jenna said.

'I thought you were an anarchist.'

'I am. You can have a job too, you know.'

'Is it a family shop, or…?'

'No, I'm just on the till. You get to learn a lot.'

'Really? I'll have to get you to date Luisa's pots.'

'Yes. I saw them. How old did you think they were?'

'Oh, I don't know. A hundred years or so?'

'Yes.' She rowed, and he listened to the sound of her breathing. 'Well,' she continued. 'I'm afraid they're quite new. Maybe ten years old.'

Robert looked at her. She smiled apologetically. 'There's a lot of it about these days. Put a yellowing glaze on it. Chip a bit off the rim and stick it back together with glue that yellows. Put some dust in the bottom. How much did you pay for them?'

'Oh, er, well, not much.'

'I hope it wasn't more than a fiver.' She sniffed. 'They're quite pretty I suppose.'

VI

In the centre of the lake, Jenna let the oars rest on the edge of the boat and laid herself along the seat, her head on one lip of the boat and her feet dangling over the other. Robert heard the oars and the wood of the boat resonate, in the way things sound distinct and clear when the weather is hot.

Luisa and Jay had disappeared. Robert thought about Hitler's jaw. Even if it is his, why queue up to look at a bit of skull anyway? You know what it's going to look like. Why does the fact that it's Hitler's make you look into a glass case and feel something going up and down your spine? But it does... for some reason Hitler's jaw is different.

Jenna closed her eyes. Robert watched her chest rise and fall. Her feet gently tapped against the side of the boat. They did not quite reach the water. She had silver toenail polish like Luisa. The soles of her feet were black.

Robert rooted around on the floor of the boat and found *Dream Story*. He opened it in the middle and read a passage at random.

> 'Take off your mask!' cried several of them at once. Fridolin held up his arm in front of him as if to shield his face. It seemed to him a thousand times worse to stand there as the only one unmasked amid a host of masks, than suddenly to stand naked among those fully dressed. And in a firm voice he said –

The sun was strong on the page and Robert had to squint. The pages flickered in the breeze and he held his hand against them. The book was as hot and as white as Luisa's bedroom that morning. His eyes started to skip lines and he felt drowsy. He closed his eyes for a moment and the book fell into the boat without him realising he'd dropped it. Jenna opened her eyes, looked up at him and pulled herself upright. The boat was floating almost without moving in the centre of the lake.

'So why haven't I met you before?' she said.

He shrugged. 'I haven't been up to London.'

'Why not?'

He watched her face move back and forth as she started rowing again. He let the silence run on between them, like trickling water.

'You can tell me, you know.'

'There was a girl I was going out with. Ann, she was called.' His voice sounded unfamiliar, as if he were in a radio play.

'And?'

'And she died. She was killed. In a car. She died in a car. In an accident.'

Jenna rowed. 'Did you love her?'

'Yes. Very much.'

She put the oars down. The boat floated gently.

'It's kind of made me what I am. It's why I'm a bit unfriendly. I'm sorry about that. I didn't go out for a long time. That's why I haven't seen Luisa for a year.'

Jenna nodded. She picked up the oars again. They passed near the bank and Jenna's face sparkled green. 'I was really rude to you last night,' he said. 'I'm sorry.'

Jenna smiled. 'But now you've started going out again.'

'Yes. I wish I'd done it before.' His voice changed; its pitch raised a note or so. 'I've never taken a boat out on a lake before. Can you believe that?' Taking a boat out on a lake was something he associated with childhood; with Topsy and Tim books; with things other people did that he never did; with being alive in ways that he wasn't a part of.

'Come up and visit us next week.'

He listened to the water flowing past the boat and closed his eyes. He nodded, then shook his head as well. He opened his eyes again. Jenna had picked up the book and was flicking through it.

Conversations with Magic Stones

'I don't read novels,' she said. 'Nothing real ever happens in them. I just always know that I'm reading words on a page that someone has made up. I can never deal with that. Knowing the people aren't real.'

'I've never thought about it like that,' he said, feeling that he should say something.

'I mean it's awful. When you get to the end of the story, the people suddenly just – disappear. I can't bear that. It's really upsetting that they cease to exist; it's like they die when the story ends. What an awful fate – not to be really alive, and then to just vanish.'

'Right.' He looked at her red hair shining in the sun.

Yes, he thought, it would be pretty terrible to be a character in a story, living your life in blissful ignorance and not knowing that you're on the last page and about to vanish into nothingness. He felt grateful he was real. He lay back in the boat and looked across the lake, and saw Jay and Luisa. They too had let the oars rest on the edge of the boat, and were slowly spinning in the water. Jay had leant forward and was holding Luisa in his arms.

Robert looked down into the water. In the stillness of the centre of the lake, he saw a perfectly formed reflection. For a moment he thought it was Ann.

Ann as she had been when he first met her – when they were at school – with her hair still long, shining gold. Ann with that slightly quizzical expression on her face. Ann with her mouth a little open and looking as if she was about to speak. Ann considering carefully before she spoke, and eventually saying nothing.

The reflection re-formed into Robert's face and body, looking down into the water. Another redheaded duck swam past, causing a few ripples and making the reflection float up and down slightly, like a warped film being projected.

Robert ran a hand through the water. Next to his reflection, he saw Jenna's arm reach across and touch his face. He saw her kiss him on the cheek, then push her face across to kiss him on the lips. The reflection of her face bobbed next to his. He stared at the serene image of two faces looking down into the darkness of the lake. As he put his hand in and splashed the cool water, the image gradually broke up and disappeared into chaos.

conversations with magic stones

I

She shook me awake and bounced up and down on the bed next to me. She sucked on my finger, eventually letting it go with a fluid pop. 'We must get up,' she said. 'They'll stop serving breakfast.' But I was pressed up hard against her and we found ourselves falling backwards onto the bed, her crouching over me like a spider.

Looking down across the flat plain of my own body, seeing her two hanging breasts sway slightly above me, I reached out and gently held them as if tugging pears from a tree. She slipped her head through my hands like a horse throwing off its harness, and slid her face down onto my prick, which throbbed and pulsed inhumanly, like the body of a beheaded animal. Taking this into her mouth with a primal, guttural croak, she sucked and slid her mouth back and forth wetly, gasping as if in pain. The edges of my vision became blurred, her hair draped occasionally over the pit of my stomach and she used her fingernails to run prickles and shivers of excitement over my thighs and buttocks.

As we ate breakfast the sun broke across the dark green sheet of the sea, making points of light flash and sparkle across the water like on the surface of a quartz.

I knew nothing about her and preferred it that way. At a guess I would say she was the youngest girl I've ever taken on holiday – about twenty-three I think – and she was certainly the thinnest, wriggling and melting under my thick heavy hands like an eel. When I squeezed her middle she shivered, being ticklish there, and her stomach would contract and her jeans – size ten but hanging off her – would sag open. Momentarily I would be able to see the top of her knickers, knickers so tiny that when she rolled them down her legs and kicked them off her feet, they almost vanished. I held her now, standing on the beach at St. Ives, and pressed my thumbs against her stomach. It caved in under my touch. I ran a thumb over her belly button, feeling the contours of her skin, running in and out of the tiny, end-of-balloon knot, feeling my hand rise and fall softly like the sea as she breathed.

When she took her trousers off, she caved her legs in and kept her thighs together. She took her knickers down gently, smiled, and tossed them lightly towards me. They touched my face for a moment and I breathed in, then they slid smoothly to the floor.

I ran my hands over her body which was sculpted and elastic. There was no blemish or imperfection. I spent hours examining her for marks, but there were none. I handled her as if she were

Conversations with Magic Stones

porcelain, for fear of leaving fingerprints or bruises. She shivered when I touched her and clamped her eyes shut. There were no lines on her eyelids, even when she screwed them up.

On the beach she asked me to hold her gloves and she ran towards the sea. Against a block of sand and a block of blue, I watched a small grey figure turn a cartwheel. She came running back up the beach to me, her footprints materialising and dematerialising softly in the wet sand. Her face was red with excitement. 'I always do a cartwheel on every beach I visit,' she said breathlessly. Her mouth closed perfectly around the white, chiselled teeth.

As we walked back up the beach and the sand became dryer, she reached down and picked up a pebble. There were hardly any stones on the beach and we both noticed this particular one before she picked it up. She studied it. It was uneven and had a small hole bored through the middle. 'I'll keep this,' she said. She panted as we walked quickly towards the sea wall. 'I collect stones from beaches, don't you?'
I shook my head.
'Everyone should collect stones. It reminds you that you're part of the world.'

I like not knowing where someone comes from, or what they do, or where they're going next. I watched the sea come in and go out, inevitably, eternally, and it seemed right – it was right in itself, there was no need to ask it questions. Jessica was Jessica, and there was no need to ask her questions either. I looked at the sea. It was like a slab of blue marble.

In the warming afternoon light her face shone as if varnished. One corner of her mouth turned up and her eyes darted back and forth as she looked at each of my eyes in turn. I said nothing. She snaked a cold hand under my jumper and ran it up my back, digging her nails into my skin on the way back down. I shivered, and felt the nails scratch. She drew a stab of blood. I felt it trickle on my skin and absorb into the shirt.

II

The sky was a pewter liquid poured into the valley of two cliffs. The rock cracked as if struck by a chisel. Her arm forged across my vision like a piston, and I glanced across at the sea. Huge white collars of foam crashed and fought amongst each other in the jade water. Above the waves seagulls hovered, blown backwards from time to time, at which they squawked in alarm.

Jessica tugged at my arm and skipped across the street, running across the path of a Transit van which, although it probably wouldn't have hit her, braked in alarm. I followed sedately, smiling apologetically at the driver who wondered what I was smiling at. Opposite, she led me to a small door in a building. It looked like someone's house. Jessica quickly opened the door and pulled me inside.
The space opened up and I found myself in a large open room. A few people walked slowly back and forth. There was a faint humming in the air, as if from a large extractor fan, and a faint

Conversations with Magic Stones

smell of dust, or coal. Jessica nudged me and asked for some money. A middle-aged man milled about, his hands behind his back.

'Where are we?'

She led me up a creaking wooden staircase and I looked around. Growing from the floor like plants were the most wonderful, beautiful sculptures. Jessica walked about happily, looking at all of them quickly in turn to begin with, then concentrating on one at a time. The floor creaked and sighed under her soft steps. She ran her hands lovingly over a smooth, rounded form. It was made of wood, not varnished but polished by carving to such a fine degree that it shone. 'Touch it,' she said, 'it feels fantastic.'
'I don't think you're supposed to touch them,' I said.
She rolled her eyes at me. 'Of course you're not supposed to touch them,' she said, 'as far as the *museum* is concerned. But *she* wants you to touch them.'
'Who does?'
'Hepworth, you idiot!'
'Oh. Right. Does she?'
'Of course she does. You do *know* about Barbara Hepworth, don't you?'
Jessica ran her hands over the oval, egg-like wooden sculpture. 'It's very important to be tactile with them, that's the whole point. The desire to touch is one of the earliest human instincts. Perhaps the most important.'

Gingerly I reached out and ran a chaste hand over the round sculpture. My hand slid across much more quickly than I expected. I reached both hands out and planted them firmly but gently on the rounded slope, as if holding a child's head. Jessica smiled at me.

She held my hand and led me to another work. Spherical, made of wood, with a painted white inside. The wood was carved so that there was a curved edge folding round inside the hollowed area. It looked like a semi-peeled apple. The outside of the rind was left unpainted to enhance the impression. Where the rind ran out, seven strings were strung from the lip to the main body of the sphere. The effect of this was to make the heavy lip appear to want to pull away from the body. The strings were taut and the body seemed to resist the lip's pull.

I stood absorbing this. I imagined the sculpture without the strings, and realised it would just look like a sphere with a fluted shape emerging from it. The tightness of the strings gave a palpable tension; it looked like the sculpture would leap apart at any moment. I reached forward and cupped my hands around its base, trying to make it less tense.

III

She lay naked in bed next to me, utterly absorbed in her book. At one point she lazily raised a leg and delicately scratched the nail of her big toe against the inner thigh of the other leg. She was oblivious to me, who stared intently at this action. She sighed from time to time while she read. I lay next to her, breathing her in, doing nothing. At one point I reached across and touched her small breast, moving it gently and rhythmically. It shaped itself like wet sand, sweeping into the form my hand cupped, dropping back and moulding into Jessica again when I let go.

Lying beside me, she opened her legs and I studied the smooth, slightly indented pit below her stomach and then the fine blonde hairs that grew like marram grass on sand. Trembling slightly, on an irresistible impulse I leant over and in one solid movement licked the length of her cunt. The second time I licked it, it was wet and my tongue disappeared inside, her hair pressing up against my nose. She sighed contentedly. She smelt of the cotton of her knickers, and of the freshness of the beach. I saw her smiling at me after doing her cartwheel, red in the face and happy, and throwing her head back and smelling the salt in the sea and the fresh bracing air.

Turning away from the sculptures, Jessica twisted a loop of hair coyly around her finger, and opened her mouth for a moment, hesitating before speaking. 'Shall we look in the garden?'

IV

As if emerging through the back of a wardrobe, I blinked for a few moments in the sunlight. Strange twisting shapes rose from the ground as if stretching in the morning. Thin spirals of bronze wound intricately about each other, as if they had grown in the night. Stone shapes evolved from the wood and grass around them, flowering upright like huge mushrooms. These outside forms were larger, more primal, bolder. The pieces inside were smaller, with more attention to detail, more delicately created. Feminine works. Out here they were more roughly hewn, broader in scope, less worried about precision. Masculine. Jessica, sighing in delight, took her shoes off to walk on the grass.

It seemed to be accepted out here that you could touch the sculptures. This was part of the magic of the garden. By being outside, the pieces were removed from the safe womb of the house, where rules and instructions could exist. Here, the monuments were open to the elements; birds could land on them, insects could crawl all over them. It was impossible to feel cautious about touching them. One rounded bronze had an inner rim which had filled with rainwater, and was in common use as a birdbath. We ran our hands lovingly over the objects. Strangers walked round smiling at each other – we were all friends in this fantasy kingdom – and everyone touched, everyone felt the cold metal and stone under their fingers.

Dominating the garden was a structure consisting of monumental bronze squares, piled on top of each other like a constructivist climbing frame. It was called Four-Square (Walk-through). So we did, holding hands as we went and listening to the fabric of the sculpture echo hollowly around us.

I enjoyed the feeling of running my hand along the rough bronze interior and listening to the faint ringing sound all around me that this movement created. I was surprised at how rough the bronze was compared with the sculptures inside the house, which were polished to such a fine degree. Just as I thought this, I felt a stabbing pain in my finger and pulled my hand away sharply, examining it. The soft pads of my fingers were grazed and spotted with blood. I touched the sharp burr of the bronze again, almost in wonder.

We emerged baptismally from the other side. 'So much more fulfilling than just standing there looking at a sculpture,' murmured Jessica. 'To walk through it – to become part of it.'

Full of these shapes dotted about apparently at random, the garden looked down towards the bay of St. Ives and the nearby church, its clock face turned directly at us as if it had been designed to be seen from the garden. In this faintly unreal setting it was just another stone structure emerging from its earth.

V

She pushes my legs apart and crawls into the space they create. She snuggles against me then shifts round so that we are both face up. I sit up against the headboard to get more comfortable and shove a pillow into the pit of my back. She shuffles up the bed towards me, so we are both sitting. I kiss her shoulder blade. She reaches across to the little table and hands me the razor. I stare at it for a moment, and feel the same slight thrill of danger and excitement that I felt the first time I held one aged thirteen, and have not felt since.

She stays very still and I reach down, past the fur on her stomach. Her head is close against mine and I breathe in the gentle feminine smell of her shampoo.

She shows me exactly where to start – it's not as simple as you

might think – and, desperately hoping that my hand will stay still, I move the razor in one steady upward movement. Dark blonde filaments of hair drop away onto the white sheet. Suddenly erotically charged, she rubs her head against mine and bites my ear. 'Be careful. I don't want to cut you.'
I move across slightly, like someone lining his mower up to create straight lines in the garden, and scrape away another inch-wide section of hair. I get faster the third time, becoming more proficient at the job. I even flick the razor casually and twist it confidently in my hand.
She sighs, and slides her legs up and down on the sheet. I run a final stroke of the razor and sit back to admire my handiwork.
'Hmm,' she says, 'not bad for a first attempt.' Frowning, I notice a single hair, less than a millimetre long, that has escaped the razor. I carefully smooth it away with the blade.
She slides herself into a tiny pair of knickers. She runs her hand across the front, which is smooth and precise now, not showing up the imperfect crinkle of hair as it did before.

VI

We stood on the threshold of the summer house. There were virgin sculptures inside – the unfinished, the work-in-progress. Material she was working on at her death; half-completed ghosts of works, some barely more than rough blocks of stone.
Jessica strode in, her re-shod feet clicking on the paving stones. A bronze caught my eye. It was burnished a strong green, and I instinctively looked up to see if the clear plastic roof was leaking. The sculpture had a horizontal lip like a conch shell along its lower body. I ran my hands along it, sensing it rise and fall under my touch. It was like feeling the side of a violin.

Conversations with Magic Stones

When I looked round at Jessica, she was bending over another sculpture. Her jumper had ridden up her back and her jeans were sagging at the valley of her buttocks. Her gleaming pale flesh shone in the vague sunlight. I moved my head slightly from side to side, watching the shine move back and forth over the curve of her back.

'Look at these,' Jessica said softly, moving along. Her voice echoed around the hollow outhouse, sounding faintly unreal, synthesised.

I walked over to her. She was looking at the plants that lined the window sill; cacti mostly.

I ran my hands along the smooth pit in the small of her back, and felt the tiny blonde hairs prickling under my touch.

'They must have been here for years.'

She was right; the cacti were extremely old, perhaps twenty or thirty years. Some had huge tubes growing from them where you would normally expect just an arm of plant; tubes that had grown into strange, unnatural shapes, like ancient twisted tree trunks. They had wrapped and coiled in on themselves. You could trace their history by looking at how compressed they were. Suddenly, spiralled and warped lengths of cactus would become straight, smooth and cylindrical again, as they had been rearranged by someone and given more space, allowing them to grow straight. Others were attached by a bit of string to a vertical rod of wood, to make them grow more healthily.

The less well-tended shrunk and crouched about themselves like sciatic lizards; scabby green spiders. One thick tuber of dark green looked like a particularly lumpy and stubby slack penis.

One huge and beautiful plant had long tapering fingers that reached up as branches from a solid base. The fingers twisted about themselves and were rounded, almost like real fingers at the ends, complete with whorls for fingerprints.

In pots, younger cacti. Healthy pale green examples, with nodules that radiated spikes. Perfect spikes; several inches long, they were equidistantly spaced and all rose at exactly the same angle, forming the bones of a crown on each nodule.

'They look like little hairs,' breathed Jessica, 'they don't even look like spikes.' She reached out her gloved hand and touched them, then yelped and withdrew her hand quickly.

'Oww,' she squeaked, waving her hand in the air.

'Well what do you expect if you touch them?'

'I've got gloves on!'

She looked again, and pushed her small face up to them, her wide, pale blue eyes looking roundly in wonder.

'They look like the strings on the sculptures,' she murmured.

I went as if to go outside, but Jessica tugged at my arm.

'What's up?'

She half-smiled at me. 'I don't want to go.'

She sat on an empty plinth, and hugged her knees and looked around. The light was faintly green on her face. I breathed in the gorgeous, rich smell that you get in greenhouses and watched her.

I sat next to her on the plinth and she held me tightly, as if worried that she or I might fall off the planet. She reached round and, quick as a snake, kissed my neck. The kiss turned into a gentle bite. I watched, over her shoulder, her buttocks lift from the plinth. She bit more firmly into my neck. I ran a hand between her bottom and the cold stone. She pressed down onto my hand as she moved her head up to my face. Her tongue flicked like a lizard in and out of my mouth. I moved my hand, hot and cold on different sides, under her.

It was starting to get dark outside. When we left the summer house, shadows were falling from the sculptures. They gleamed ominously in the fading light. It was as if they were preparing to disappear back into the earth.

VII

I dreamt about you last night. I dreamt you were standing by the window, facing out. You were reading a book, and I wondered why you didn't sit down to read it. I walked up behind you and you smiled at me but then went back to the book. Your face was pale blue from the light outside. I rested you against the window sill and I peeled your trousers from you. A shiver of goosebumps prickled across the skin of your buttocks. These quickly vanished. I hooked a finger into your g-string. The fabric was stretchier than usual; I could pull it five or six inches away from your bottom without it being tight. I slid my finger down and tugged the knickers away from you. I knelt down behind you and kissed your bottom. I licked round until I touched the first soft blonde hairs. I pushed my tongue into you and ran it across the contours and folds, feeling the way your skin resisted in places like plastic and elsewhere gently caved in like butter. I held onto the backs of your legs, which were firm like clay. From time to time I heard you turning the pages of your book.

VIII

Everything seemed evocative of something when we got back to the hotel, though I don't know what it was evocative of. There was a plant in the hallway that sprouted energetically, life-fully, and seemed to have enormous meaning. The light switch was bigger than before, proud in its brass fitting. I took great pleasure in switching it on and off and on again.

'What are you *doing?*' asked Jessica irritably, running up the stairs.

I walked up after her and through the open door. The lintel seemed whiter, bolder, more carved than last time. Jessica switched on the shower then came back into the main room. She took her gloves off and gasped. Her face was pale blue against the evening light and the weak bulb.

I looked at her questioningly. She frowned and held her hand up in front of me. Four tiny, hair-like cactus spikes emerged from her finger. I held the finger at the base, then with the other hand carefully removed the spikes one by one between the very tip of my finger and thumb. The spikes were so fine that there was no blood. I held her finger up against the light to check I hadn't missed any, then kissed it. Jessica piled the rest of her clothes in the corner and stepped naked into the bathroom.

IX

The sea curved round the bay like a sheet of steel hammered into shape. I stood with my hands firmly on the window sill, feeling its smooth planed firmness under my fingers. The wood felt as if it were sprung; my fingers danced across it and made a hollow sound with their tapping. I concentrated on the bay, the sun glinting on it as on a scythe.
From the bathroom a steady rain, and the sound of Jessica softly singing.

She smiled coyly and put a finger in her mouth, then took it out again and twisted a blonde curl of hair round it. She came over to me submissively, her head on one side, took my hand and gently pushed one of my fingers into her mouth. She chewed contentedly, biting occasionally.

Lying in bed, she opened the postcards she had bought at the museum. One was conventionally enough called *Two Figures* but was completely abstract. The only concession to being figures was that they were upright and of roughly human proportions in terms of length and width.
'These two figures,' Jessica said slowly, '...are very much in love.'
They were made of elm, but there were cavities gouged into both of them. White painted, the insides sheered into the wood, and at a couple of points the cavities were so deep they became holes, bored right through the figures.
'They look like pebbles found on the beach,' she said.

She held my hand to her face and kissed it. I winced involuntarily. 'What're these?' she asked, pointing to the grazes on my hand. 'I scratched myself on that sculpture, you know, the one you can walk through.'
She looked up at me and for a moment I could see the different layers in her eyes. The film on the surface; behind that the colour of the iris; behind that the deep nothingness of the pupil. Just for a moment; then the light shifted or she shifted and the impression faded. She held my hand in front of her face, ran her lips along it, and kissed it, and licked it.

'I'm tired,' she murmured. She dropped the cards on the floor and rolled over to me, her eyes closed. She lay on her front and I massaged her, slowly and gently to begin with, then harder. She told me to dig my elbow into certain parts of her back, to put my whole weight into leaning on her in this way. I said she would snap, I didn't want to damage her, but she giggled at this and told me it would be good for her.
I climbed into the space between her legs, then leant fully on her and did as she asked. When she'd had enough of this, I kneaded her back, feeling her flesh bunch and fall under my grasp. I twisted her spine so she was properly straight, grasped the skin, manipulated it, watching it turn pink then white then back to its normal colour when I let go, leaping quickly back into its original shape.

She was wearing thin pink cotton knickers. I rubbed myself against her bottom, but did not remove the pants. She murmured about being sleepy, and I said not to worry, we didn't have to make love if she didn't want to, even though I wanted to be

inside her, I wanted to be part of her.
'I'm just your object,' she said quietly.
'You're not my object. You're my subject.'
She sniffed at this. 'Yes, I know what you mean. Even though you think I don't.'

I came on her knickers. I lay there, watching her perfect form. She shifted a little on the bed, which creaked, and she smiled, opened her eyes for a moment and then closed them again. After a few seconds her breathing became shallower and more regular. She slept soundly and almost silently, still on her front, her hair spread in ringlets by the side of her head, her motionless body posing for Botticelli, a porcelain arm cast across the folds and billows of the bed.

Lying face down next to her, I looked over the surf of mattress and by the wooden side of the bed saw the cards scattered on the floor. Stone and bronze gazed back up at me. My mind was turbulent and racing from thought to thought. Most of these thoughts were in one way or another to do with Jessica's body. The stone calmed me. I scratched my face and ran my hand over my nose, cheeks, chin and forehead. It was as if I was realising I had such things for the first time. It was if I had suddenly discovered there was a body, separate from me.

A hot country. Italy perhaps, or Spain. Sandstone buildings, cathedrals. Large buildings made of white stone, fluffy blobby stone, the walls looking like they're caked in icing sugar. Little rounded windows cut into the buildings, holes made in the icing by a finger. The sound of passing feet magnified on the gravel because it's so hot.

A lizard, utterly still, splayed on a white stone wall. Close up it is not motionless; its tiny chest rises and falls quickly, spasmodically. The lizard disappears into a crack in the rock in one instant movement. An enveloping warmth as the ground gets hotter and hotter. I close my eyes against the glare of the sun on the white rock.

The morning light falls into the room in beams. She picks up her pink knickers. They are stained with white; his on the outside, hers on the inside. She examines this and frowns, thinking about it. It means something, although she does not know what.
Gently – as if dropping a live animal – she lets the knickers fall in a little bundle in the corner of the room. They land artificially, with hills and bumps in them, jagged little slopes, plateaux near the top. She looks at them carefully.

An image as I come into consciousness; the last frame of dreams. Jessica, wearing only a tight pair of blue jeans, looking at me and smiling. She puts her foot up on the edge of the bed and I slowly kiss it, sucking the toe into my mouth.

x

I watched her as we walked round the corner, and as we did so her face sparkled red, then green, then blue. I turned my head forward. The arc of Mousehole harbour was lit up with gigantic,

Conversations with Magic Stones

colourful illuminations. A snowman, white bulbs twinkling and a red scarf slung across his neck. A whale, with a blue fountain of water emerging from its blowhole. The lights flashed on and off in sequence so it looked like the water was actually spouting.

Jessica ran down towards the harbour. I clumsily half-ran, half walked after her. She skipped and weaved expertly between adults moving like chess pieces and children careering like wound-up toys. I bumped into someone and apologised, then trod on some child's foot. I walked rapidly away as the child started wailing.

Jessica, her face now glowing yellow and orange, looked up at me. 'Oh it's lovely,' she said, 'thank you for bringing me here. It's a wonderful surprise!'
I grinned. 'I didn't know it was going to be like this!'
We stood on the harbour and hugged, and she gently teased her finger up and down my chest. We listened to the gentle lapping of the water in the bay.

Jessica and me, merging into each other; the shape of two heads not quite separated, rather like Siamese twins. The coloured lights made us, to the observer, a silhouette, an amorphous shape, which the eye can turn into two figures but which are actually one solid, formed object.

She squeezed my hand. Because she was cold she put both our hands into her coat pocket.

My fingers closed round hers and then round the small stone with the hole in it, which she had picked up on the beach.
Our fingers rubbed warmly against each other.
I felt the smooth, supple bone of Jessica's fingers, solid beneath the living flesh of her hand.

        Sea Form (Porthmeor) (1958)
Four-Square (Walk-Through) (1966)
            Spring 1966 (1966)
       Sea Form (Atlantic) (1964)
    Curved Form (Trevalgan) (1956)
         Two Figures (1947-8)
           Pelagos (1946)

in shape of lions

I

Siobhan stood on the bridge and looked down at the green water. 'Is that where we get the boats?' she asked.

He nodded. 'Yes, we go down those steps over there.'

'Are you any good at rowing then?'

'No, we get a punt out.'

She frowned. 'That's Cambridge, isn't it?'

'We have punts here too,' he smiled.

They walked further across the bridge. 'That's the botanical gardens over there,' he said, pointing.

She pulled a face. 'We'll go there later. I'm hungry. I'll show you a pub on the Cowley road, that's where I used to go all the time.'

'Oh. Okay. I thought you didn't know Oxford.'

'I don't know *this* bit, the bit with like all the *buildings* and stuff.'

They turned round and back across the bridge, then walked for ten minutes or so, across the roundabout, past the corner pub, and along the Cowley Road.

II

'I'll get them, as I owe you about two squillion drinks.' She went off to the bar. She had changed so much, he thought, as he watched her go. Two years ago she had been difficult, prickly, and at times explosive. He had stayed with her because she had been devastatingly, irresistibly gorgeous. In bed, she was sensational; it was an almost transcendent experience at times. He would sit on the bed in her tiny flat, drenched in sweat, smoking a cigarette, and watch her rub her foot up against his leg, push her toe seductively in his mouth and study him from deep, powerful blue eyes, a smile curling from one side of her mouth like a smirk. As she breathed heavily, he would watch her small, delicate chest move up and down.

When they made love she was fragile, stick-thin in his arms and he felt he had to be gentle or he would break her; but then she would shift position and push him up against the wall and take charge, riding him powerfully, and he was entirely in her power. He would look up at the curls of her hair bouncing against her forehead; gasping, her eyes closed, she would reach orgasm with a series of primitive, animal-like grunts that increased in volume, got higher in pitch and became shorter and shorter until they fused in a primeval cry. She would fall forward on to him like a building collapsing or a world ending. It would take several seconds for both of them to come round, and they would stare at each other in amazement and shake their heads wonderingly, expressing without words the sense of disbelief that such an experience, such *being*, could be created out of nothing.

He looked around the pub. She came back with the drinks and sat opposite him. 'I recognise a few people,' she said. 'This is where I used to go all the time when I was at school. I recognise the bloke behind the bar, anyway. I think I snogged him once.' She sipped at her pint of beer with a slurp.

'You are a very naughty girl.'

She closed her eyes and made a kissing noise with her mouth, pouting and pushing her lips outwards characteristically. It was a mannerism he loved; it made him want to lean across the table and kiss her.

'I know,' she said.

In two years she had put on weight, and although she was still beautiful, was not as impossibly physically perfect as she had been at 18. Two years of smoking and drinking had also taken their toll; her skin had its very first lines, a crease appeared in her forehead when she frowned, and her hair was not as radiant and glossy. Nickolas tapped his cigarette on the table thoughtfully as he considered these facts. Perfection is a futile objective; even if you attain it, within a few years it has started to fade. The irony is that it is only if you have been perfect, that people will notice you are not perfect any more. If you were ugly to begin with, it wouldn't matter.

He glanced up. The doorway was open behind her and rich afternoon light fell into the pub. Her hair glowed gold.

'Give us some money,' she said, 'and I'll get us another one. And they're, um, only doing roasts, but that's okay, isn't it, it's really really cheap and it's good food.'

He handed her a note. A strikingly attractive girl walked past as Siobhan crossed to the bar. She was slim and sexy and Siobhan looked back to Nickolas to see his reaction. He didn't seem to notice her to begin with; then, conscious of making an effort, he vaguely smiled at her. That's something I'm going to have to start getting the hang of again, he thought.

'She was nice,' Siobhan said when she came back. 'Not that you looked at her really obviously or anything.'

He smiled in the same vague way as he had at the girl.

'So has that cow finally left you then?' Siobhan sipped at her beer and looked up at him.

He shook his head. 'No, no, I left her.'

'Why?'

'Er – she was sleeping with lots of people. We don't have to go into it, do we?'

'No, not if you don't want to.'

She turned round in her seat to reach into her bag. As he watched, her bottom moved up and down slightly before settling. She sat back down in the seat with a bump, having found her cigarettes. 'Oh yes,' she was saying, as she lit one and took a deep drag of it. 'So, um, I meant to say, I think I might be pregnant.'

'What?'

She twisted her mouth to one side. 'Er, well, I seem to have had this comedy pregnancy moment, anyway. Well, basically we hadn't been using condoms, for one reason or another – ' she talked over the look on his face – 'and er, yeah, I didn't come on and – well, the gist being that I'd come off the pill – so, er, I, well… I did a test and it came out positive.'

He raised his eyebrows at her. Was he supposed to say 'congratulations,' or 'so what are you going to do about it?'

'But I was very drunk when I did the test,' she said, thoughtfully tapping her cigarette on the ashtray, 'maybe it wasn't the colour I thought it was, and anyway, they say that one per cent of them are wrong.'

'Right.' Nickolas looked at her and narrowed his eyes. She

looked round the pub, taking an interest in everything, watching everyone who walked past or milled about by the fruit machine. A little girl walked past, spilling a blackcurrant juice, and Siobhan raised her eyebrows and pulled a face. The little girl laughed unself-consciously, before her mother overtook her, caught her hand and whisked her away.

The meals arrived. 'It looks really good,' Nickolas said, unable to keep the surprise out of his voice. For a fiver it was enormous.

'Yeah. Well,' she said, 'if I didn't know how it was made, I would probably enjoy it more.'

She said this just as he put the first forkful into his mouth. 'Er – sorry?' he said, swallowing uncertainly. 'What do you mean?'

'Well they make them the day before, and then just heat it all up in the microwave on Sunday.'

'Oh, right,' he said, relieved. 'No problem with that; it's not going to do you any harm. How do you know all this, anyway?'

She bit into her Yorkshire pudding, which bounced soggily in her mouth. 'I used to work here.'

'Really?'

'I *told* you, I used to come here all the time at school.'

'Yes, you told me that bit, but not that you worked here…'

She nodded. 'Yeah, when I was going out with David.'

'Oh, right.' He speared four perfect circles of carrot with his fork.

'Well, technically I was going out with Ian, so David and I just spent all our time in here so that Ian wouldn't see us.'

'Right.'

The sexy girl walked past again. Siobhan nudged Nickolas with her foot.

'What?' he said, looking up. She opened her eyes wide and nodded her head to the left. He smiled at her, then turned back to Siobhan. 'So what have you been reading lately?' he asked.

'Ovid's *Metamorphoses*.'

'Oh, right.'

'Have you ever read it?'

'Er – no.' Has anyone, he wondered.

'Oh, you should. It's fantastic.' Why couldn't he have been like this two years ago, she thought; he was impossible then. He was too wrapped up in work; he always had to be getting things done; whenever they went out he wouldn't just go to the pub, it always had to be a play or a concert or some other improving event. And she had never had the money for it, and he knew that, but she did what he wanted, which she thought was rather nice of her, and then he seemed to resent the fact that he was paying for everything.

Now, she observed, he was quite happily sitting in a pub, tapping his cigarette in time with the music and looking for all the world as if he would contentedly stay there all afternoon, asking her idle questions about what she was reading and what she was doing. This is the kind of person I wanted to go out with at the time, she thought, and God, as she watched him picking at his roast beef, I still really really fancy him. And he went and bought them some wine, because he said he couldn't drink any more beer at lunchtime, and they sat there for another hour or so, talking about this and that; it was so relaxing, and so unlike how he used to be. She wondered if perhaps he'd solved his various panic issues. Certainly finally leaving the stupid old cow seemed to have done him some good.

In the end it was Siobhan who stood up and rubbed her hands together and said, 'well, we'd better get on to these botanical gardens if we're going to have a full itinerary.' This was usually his job, to get the day moving again. He nodded and got to his feet leisurely. She liked this new improved version of him. Shame it was too late. Shame she was pregnant.

He watched her as she thought all this, realising how beautiful she was and wondering why he hadn't phoned her in the last six months. It was too late now, it seemed. How long had she been with what's his name; it couldn't be that long, surely?

He felt a great increase of affection and love for her as he looked at her now. There used to be lots of things about her that weren't actually that nice; they seemed to be disappearing. She wasn't as stroppy as she used to be. When he asked her questions she didn't jump down his throat or talk as if he should know exactly what was going on in her life and get cross if she had to explain things that were, to her, obvious.

This was why he had not enjoyed his time with her as much as he should have done when they were going out; now, however, he perceived that he could do. Don't get me wrong, he told himself as he nodded slowly as she spoke; he had enjoyed the relationship very much when they were going places or having sex; he had been transfixed by her, mesmerised, and he never thought about anything else when he was with her, the time went by in a kind of trance, a free-floating, hot, sexy wildness. But when he wanted a quiet conversation, or felt like sitting on the sofa reading a book for the evening, or wanted to go for a quiet walk or have an early night, which admittedly didn't happen very often but happened occasionally, he would rush back to Elaine.

This was why sitting in a pub with her just now was enjoyable, in a way it hadn't been before. If he was meeting her for the first time now, he would want to go out with her.

Although he and Elaine stopped having sex, and were friends, it meant he had never really left her, in his mind. When he split up with Siobhan, neither he nor Siobhan were convinced that splitting up was the right thing to do; he just knew he couldn't be with her. They still wanted to see each other and they still desired each other, but Nickolas wasn't surprised that Siobhan had difficulties adjusting to the fact that he still saw Elaine. She was young, and the idea of staying friends with a former partner was alien to her. Not to mention inherently suspicious.

For her part, Siobhan was not surprised that he had gone back to Elaine when they had split up. She never believed they had stopped having sex in the first place.

III

She smiled pleasantly at the woman in the little hut. 'One and a student,' she said.

Nickolas rubbed his cheek. That familiar expression, that he hadn't heard since the last time he had gone up to Edinburgh to see her. The castles they had visited, tramping across fields to get there, her frustrated and tired, wet and muddy and cold, but indulging him, wanting to traipse through fields to reach broken down ruins because he wanted to. Then saying to the person in the hut when they got there, breathless and her wet hair dripping into her mouth, and her cheeks flushed, 'One and a student'. It was like an incantation; a group of words that had mystical significance.

The woman nodded and asked to see Siobhan's card. She handed it over and opened her furry handbag. It was a bag

Nickolas had bought for her; she had seen it in a shop and said she loved it, but didn't have enough money for it. It was only ten pounds or something, but she said she couldn't afford things she didn't really need.

He nodded and approved of her recognition that she had to sensible with money. This would have been just before they'd gone to the pub for the evening and each spent about twenty pounds getting tremendously drunk.

Nickolas thought that the bag was silly and frivolous, and couldn't imagine why she would want such a thing. The next day he walked back to Princes Street and bought it for her.

'No,' said the woman in the hut, frowning and handing Siobhan's card back.

'What? What do you mean no?'

'It's not a card we can accept.'

'It's a student card. It's an NUS card. I'm a student from the University of Edinburgh, what do you mean you can't accept it?' She fell over her words and pouted as she spoke; Nickolas watched silently, remembering how wound up she would get by authority, by unfairness; the way she would start pointing out things that meant nothing to the person listening. Emphasising the university she was at was irrelevant to the sour-faced old woman sitting in front of them. Siobhan just appeared arrogant and pushy.

'Yes,' said the woman patiently, 'but it's not an *Oxford* student card.' She waved her arm proprietarily over a laminated sheet of paper that showed the cards that were acceptable.

'But I'm a student,' Siobhan said, her insistent voice wavering.

The woman shrugged and looked down at her till. These youngsters think they own the place, Nickolas could see her thinking. Well, she thought as her lips contracted, I'll show her. Nickolas silently handed over a twenty pound note.

'And they wonder why people think that Oxford is snobbish,' Siobhan said loudly, as Nickolas took his change and they walked away from the woman, who avoided eye contact with either of them. How absurd and elitist, Nickolas agreed, that the student discount only applied to Oxford students.

They walked past the peaceful ponds with the trickling fountains and the vast plants with what looked like huge rhubarb leaves, and along the narrow, winding paths filled with sweet-smelling, brightly-coloured flowers. The plants spilled over into the pathways. Nickolas ran his fingers along the veined leaves and the soft, furry petals of flowers.

They emerged into a little circular area of thick, mossy grass, secluded by overhanging bushes and small stone walls. They stood for a moment, breathing in huge lungfuls of the scented air. 'You look around when it's like this,' she said, 'and you see the trees, and these beautiful plants, and the water cascading over the stones in the ponds, and you really feel God's presence.'

'Mmm.'

'I mean, people who don't believe in God, I just want to bring them somewhere like this.' She looked up at him, her eyes wide and innocent. 'It would soon make them change their minds, wouldn't it?'

'Yes,' he murmured. She looked at him. Neither of them said anything else. They continued walking and held the vulnerable leaves of the plants in their hands. Branches and flowers brushed their faces.

'Wow, look at these, what are these called?'

Nickolas's glasses steamed up the moment they entered the

greenhouse. He took his glasses off and peered myopically at the plant she was enthusiastically indicating.

'Er – I don't know.' Beads of sweat instantaneously formed over his neck and chest. He shivered and wriggled as the sweat ran down his back in rivulets and gathered at the base of his spine.

'So what are *these* called?' She led him further along the path and pointed at something that looked, through his misty glasses, like any of the other big plants.

'Er – I don't know.' Another thing he didn't know was why she assumed he would know everything. She seemed to have endless faith in his knowledge, without making the effort to learn anything herself.

Eventually he started surreptitiously reading the names on the little plastic pegs that were stuck into the soil. He told her each time she asked, and each time she was really impressed. He wondered how long it would take her to spot the pegs. She didn't.

His shirt clung to his armpits and his arms developed goosebumps. 'So anyway,' she said as they walked along, 'I did this pregnancy test thingy, and okay I was a bit drunk, but it definitely turned the colour that it turns if you're pregnant. So maybe that means it *is* true.'

She stopped mid-step, as if considering the reality of it for the first time.

'Well, yes,' he said uncomfortably, looking at her carefully to see how she would react, 'of course you are.' He wiped his glasses, which were finally beginning to adjust to the moisture in the air.

She looked up at him, those innocent blue eyes less happy. He shrugged. 'Sorry to be harsh about it. You've got to face up to it, you know?'

She chewed her lip, and tasted salt from her sweat; it tasted as if she had been crying.

'There's no doubt about it, is there?' he continued. 'You *are* pregnant, there's no "I think I *might* be pregnant." '

'Look! Wow – look, these are Venus fly traps! I always thought they were made up, I didn't know they were real. Look, they're tiny, I always thought they were supposed to be huge, you know, great man-sized things.'

He looked down at the plants, which sat gapingly open, blindly waiting for their next meal. There was a gauze with flies crawling upside-down on the inside; the plant keepers evidently tipped the flies in here, dooming them to the terrifying fate of being clamped between the fleshy, spiky pads. The fly traps looked like huge red thighs, waiting to crush some helpless creature's head.

They moved on. 'So...' he said, somewhat anxiously, 'what are you going to do, you're... you seem very laid back about it.'

She shrugged and fingered the leaves of a plant with orange flowers. 'Well, it's still not definite, is it. I mean sometimes these tests go wrong, they're not a hundred per cent. No point worrying about it till then.'

'Er well, no, they're not a hundred per cent.' He studied her. 'But they are ninety-nine per cent.'

She shrugged again. 'So mine could be one of the one per cent that are wrong.' He sighed, exasperated at her young, naïve way of looking at things. 'I might buy another test today. Do you think Boots is open on a Sunday?'

He pursed his lips and tried to think of what to say, but anything he thought of would potentially annoy her and make her angry; the old Siobhan might come back. She was peering with intent at a banana plant, a childlike look of wonder on her face. She looked at it with fascination, amazed that something as familiar as a banana could actually grow on a tree. 'It's incredible, isn't it,' she said, 'the way they grow like berries.'

'That's because,' he told her, 'believe it or not, they actually are berries.'

She refused to accept this and frowned crossly at him. 'Of course they're not berries,' she said, looking at him as if he should know better. 'They're bananas.'

At the top were unformed, flaccid green tiny banana-shaped embryos, that would develop into the full yellow ones that hung further down. They looked like chillies. Lower still were brown, dead ones, as shrivelled as the undeveloped ones.

Her test, he thought, was the kind of thing he had found difficult to deal with in the old days; the way she seemed so unconcerned about anything important. This was a major issue, and she didn't seem remotely bothered by it. She didn't even seem to believe it was happening. She had convinced herself that the test could be wrong; he shook his head in surprise at her casual attitude to it.

'These are amazing.' She held a banana tenderly in her hand.

'Do you think you should still be smoking?' he said, frowning at her, 'haven't you thought of that?'

'Do you think anyone would mind if I picked one?'

'Or drinking so much?'

She shrugged. 'Oh, I'm sure if it's survived the last few days, it'll survive another one.'

He looked at her aghast. She held on to the banana and waggled the plant up and down. The leaves flapped and created a breeze.

She looked at him. 'Don't *worry*,' she said, closing her eyes momentarily and shaking her head, 'I'll stop if it's proved definite.'

He drew in breath.

'But it isn't proved, is it, I keep *telling* you, it might be wrong. I'm not going to give myself a nightmare day not smoking if I don't have to.' She wiped her forehead. 'I'll make an appointment with the doctor tomorrow.'

But, he thought anxiously, you *are* pregnant. And every day you carry on smoking –

'And there's *hundreds* of them,' she said, smiling at the bananas as if they were small children.

He wasn't sure why she was denying it so completely; she seemed to be consciously ignoring its reality. It was just her way of dealing with it, he supposed. Maybe this is a good thing, that she *can* deal with it. He wondered what she would be like when it sank in.

It had been like this when they were going out; he would often point something out to her and she would simply deny it, even when it was obviously true. He didn't exactly intend to be always right; but the fact was that he usually was right.

This wasn't false pride and he was only running the idea through his head; but something reacted inside him and told him, 'you're being arrogant.' It was as if he could hear someone listening to his inner monologue and saying it to him. He wouldn't say it to anyone else, after all, so why did he feel guilty for thinking it?

He sighed. 'I mean okay they say a chance but… really… we know…' he looked at her sincerely and she frowned. She tossed her hair petulantly. 'Anyway, I don't want to talk about it any more.'

That was always the last response. 'Okay,' he murmured.

She walked ahead of him for a few steps and onto a bridge with wooden slats that creaked under her feet.

Conversations with Magic Stones

'Well,' he said, trying to be optimistic, 'perhaps you're right, perhaps you... messed the test up or something.'

She turned back to look at him. 'What – I might have pissed on the stick wrongly?'

He followed her across the bridge and shrugged. Siobhan grinned. 'Anyway, I'll get another testy thing, do you think Boots will be open on a Sunday?' He shook his head. He had learned to be patient with the way she would ask questions and a few minutes later ask them again as if she hadn't said them the first time.

'It'll wait till tomorrow, won't it?' he said. 'I mean if you *are*, it's not going to make any difference to things.'

They carried on walking, and he watched her, and she was amazing. He would go out with her now, he decided. Now that she was pregnant. He sighed. He was in love with her after all. Yes, she could be a headache. But he would put up with that, now that he had finally left Elaine. When he was going out with Siobhan, Elaine had seemed calm and stable and in comparison Siobhan was histrionic and draining.

When Siobhan was back from university for the long holidays, she had always wanted to go out every night. She would ring him at work at about three in the afternoon and complain about having what she described as 'cabin fever' from being at her parents' house all day. And she would ask him to go straight round after work, and they would go out about half past six, and eat, and then go to a pub till eleven, and Nickolas would end up paying for most of it. And then at half past eleven she would want to go to a club. And he would look at his watch and grimace, and think, I've got to get up for work at eight.

So by about Thursday, he was shattered, and could barely keep his eyes open at work. When he said he was tired and didn't really want to go out, she would say, 'oh you're so *boring*'; but if he rang her without thinking before about midday, she would complain that she was asleep, tell him to ring her back at a less ungodly hour and put the phone down.

So he had gone running back to Elaine because although Siobhan was exciting, she was too exciting. He wanted a calmer, quieter life. But now that there wasn't an Elaine anyway, Siobhan seemed thrilling and stimulating again. Looking back, Elaine was dull and boring. Siobhan had calmed down a lot. Nickolas scratched his head. Have I finally made my mind up, he wondered, feeling the same sense of guilt as before; the feeling that someone was hearing the thoughts inside his head and telling him to get a grip.

She looked in wonder at some beautiful red and yellow flowers with spikes sticking out from them. He enjoyed her childlike sense of joy with the world, the youthful, innocent delight in being that had not yet disappeared, and which he hoped never would.

Unlike Siobhan, looking at these plants made him realise that there couldn't be a God. Nickolas saw life as random and accidental, and wherever Siobhan saw a pattern to indicate a creator, Nickolas saw the human brain seeing patterns that did not exist. We see faces in clouds or in the fire, and to Nickolas this proved that humans want to see shapes and meaning where in fact there is nothing.

The reason we see shapes where none exist is because this is how we survived when we were animals. If you can see two points of light and infer a predator, you can jump out of the way. The animals that had these skills were the ones that survived, and so we are descended from them. The animals that did not have such skills died out, so there are no descendants who don't see patterns in things. Ergo, most people around today are people who believe in God; because they are pattern-seeing people. The non-pattern-seeing people got eaten by predators, so there aren't so many people around who do not see patterns and interpret meaning from them.

This was an instinct deep within him, and as he touched the leaf of a plant and ran his nail across the veins he shuddered. I don't see God here, he thought, I see plants evolving; blind life reaching out and existing for the sake of existing, not knowing why and not even knowing that they don't know. There's just survival. Again, the ones that aren't bothered by surviving die out. So everywhere we see life, thriving and wanting to live. That doesn't mean there's a God behind them though. It's just that the ones that don't have that blind drive, aren't here.

Why did he have such lust for Siobhan, for example? If there is a God, you don't need lust. It's evolved simply because the creatures that enjoy sex will create lots of descendants, and pass these sex-loving genes on to them. So you end up with lots of randy people running round wanting to have sex with lots of other randy people. The people who don't enjoy sex die out. Siobhan would argue against this that you can look round and see plenty of people who don't enjoy sex.

To which Nickolas would respond, yes, it might take a few thousand years to have an effect. Taking a snapshot of this precise moment of time will always show anomalies. But after another few hundreds of thousands of years of evolution, people will be even sexier and there will be no non-sexy people left. The irony is that then, because people believe in God, they beat themselves up about feeling sexy; they believe it's 'bad' in some way.

Now a God isn't going to invent all that. There's no *need* for it. He rubbed the leaf of a banana plant and held an unripe, unformed banana in his hand.

IV

They walked back in the direction of the bridge. 'Are those new glasses?' she said.
'Yes.'
'Wow, look, they've gone all – like all *dark*.'
'Yes, they've got these lenses in them that darken in the sun.'
'Wow.' She looked at him in wonder. She held her hands up in front of his face, to see if they went back to normal again. He stumbled and walked into her hand.
'Sorry.'
'So,' he said, 'if you'd come off the pill, how did you manage to... I mean, weren't you careful?'
She shrugged. 'Well, we were planning not to.'
'Not to...?'
'Not to... you know.'
'Oh, *right*,' he said, comprehending. 'Right. I see. That's not like you.'
She grinned. 'I know. But, you know, we wanted to do it properly. He wanted to be a *proper* Christian. He's the first person I've ever loved, you see. So I've been wanting to wait for the right moment.'
He nodded. He bit his lip at the way she unconsciously communicated things to him. He nodded again as she lit another cigarette and scratched at the skin under her shoulder blades, just above the dip of her breasts. When she took her fingers away there were three red marks on the skin.
'So,' he said, 'in the end you didn't wait.'
'Er – no. And it was *fantastic*.'

Conversations with Magic Stones

'So why didn't you use anything?'

'Oh, well I forgot, I mean I've been on the... you know, for years.'

On the bridge she stopped, grabbed hold of him and kissed his neck. She pushed her teeth up against his skin, bit him hard, and twisted his skin in her mouth. He winced and closed his eyes tight, and the world went black and disappeared for a moment, as it always did when she did this. He lost sensation in his limbs and felt as if he was floating off the ground. It was like being on a fairground ride – the world travelled past quickly and noisily, each of his limbs tightened up and there was the stomach-lifting sense of careering out of control through the air.

She set him back down again and looked at him carefully. 'The sun's gone in,' she said, 'but your glasses are still dark.'

'Mmm.'

'I always used to love biting you.' She put her arm through his as they walked along. 'I suppose I'm going to have to stop doing that now. Which is a shame.' She looked up at him and narrowed her eyes. 'I like *branding* you,' she said. 'So I know you're mine.'

He nodded. 'Well – '

'I mean,' she interrupted, 'I still care for you very very much and we're still going to have our great days out.'

'Yes.'

'But I'm happy now.'

He nodded. 'Good. Good.'

They stood and looked down towards the botanical gardens again. 'They seem smaller now we're not in them,' she commented.

'Yes. That's because they're further away.'

They stood in silence. The stream of cars was steady but after a few moments they didn't notice them any more; it was as if the bridge were empty and quiet. The background noise had become normality.

'I suppose I still miss her,' he said eventually. 'I suppose I love her. I think so.'

'No, no,' she said, 'this is a good thing, it's good for you, it's great. This is really exciting. You can go out and shag lots of sexy girls.'

'Yes, right.'

She grabbed his hand and dragged him further along the bridge. 'I'm so glad we've stayed friends,' she said.

'Me too.'

'Also ... I've got some news for you.'

She grinned at him, a broad grin that he remembered from when they had gone out. She would keep her head still, look at him through her hair and open her mouth wide, Cheshire cat-like, a full beam like a lighthouse.

'Yes...' he said, dubiously, nervously, fearing the worst.

'Look.' As she held her finger up in front of him, the ring glittered more brightly than the smile.

He nodded thoughtfully. It was turning out to be an eventful day.

V

He put his hand in the water and let it trail along.

'Try it,' he said, 'it's really nice.'

She put her hand in the water.

'Actually,' he said, thinking about it, 'it's bloody freezing.'

They opened the wine. It wasn't proper wine, it was a kind of fizzy, 5 per cent stuff. Siobhan raised an eyebrow at Nickolas as they drank the first mouthful from a plastic cup. But, after they had downed it and drunk a second cup, it didn't seem so bad.

They tried to make conversation with the boatman. It had been Siobhan's idea to get a chauffered one. Nickolas had been all for punting it himself, but she had frowned and said 'but that way you don't get to *relax*.'

He nodded. This was one of his problems, enjoying himself; she had always claimed he wasn't very good at it. So he nodded. 'Yes. Right.' It cost twice as much to get a chauffeur, for half the time you would get on your own, but as Siobhan pointed out, you get a free bottle of wine. 'So that makes it about the same really.'

He didn't quite follow this logic but nodded and followed her. He drank the sparkling shitzenhocken and sat back and let the world take him where it wanted to take him. He pointed towards a bridge they were slowly moving past.

'Last time I was here,' he said to the boatman, 'I think I punted past that bridge. Is that the bit where it goes on for about a mile and then it comes to a dead end and you have to try to turn round?'

The boatman nodded, blowing smoke out through his nose and half-closing his eyes. 'Yeah. We often find stranded Italians up there at the end of the day, when we've forgotten about them for hours and they've got stuck there and don't know what to do.'

Siobhan laughed.

'Why don't they put signs up to say, don't go down there?'

'We can't.'

'Why not?'

The man shrugged and blew more endless smoke from his nostrils. 'We're not allowed to.'

Nickolas nodded and stopped talking. He felt that he was

always referring to things he had done in the past; that he was being boring. It was *now*, he told himself, forget about the past, enjoy now, this moment. He looked at Siobhan.

Opposite him, looking into his eyes, she wondered why he had broken off the anecdote and was frowning. She had been enjoying listening to him, taking pleasure in hearing what he had to say. She was enjoying the feeling of it being now. He was so different. She loved him. It was a bit annoying.

'So,' he said, as they turned a bend in the river and some ducks swam away from them, quacking in alarm, 'you saw God in the botanical gardens.'

She lit two cigarettes, leant forward and pushed one of them into his mouth. 'Yeah,' she said, blowing smoke into the air, 'didn't you?'

'Well – no, not really.' The wine had emboldened him. It was horrible stuff, but was still having an effect, probably because it was three o'clock in the afternoon and they had had several beers in the pub.

'You've got lots of issues with God, haven't you,' she said, trailing her hand in the water. It didn't seem so cold now.

'Oh, yeah. I mean....' He looked around, searching for an example. 'September 11th,' he said eventually.

'Yes?' She looked at him, ready to argue and not worried by anything he might say. It was like playing chess with her; they both enjoyed the battle. They used to play strip chess – the rules of which they had invented themselves one drunken afternoon in her room. An item of clothing for every piece, and everything if your queen was taken. They were also very competitive at pool. Siobhan had always been disappointed that they couldn't play strip pool, because she was better at pool than chess.

'How can God exist,' he said, 'and allow something like September 11th to happen? Or,' he said, wanting to clarify things, as she opened her mouth to reply – 'how can he be an all-powerful God, which we're supposed to believe he is, and also a merciful God, which we're also supposed to believe he is, and allow that kind of thing to happen?'

Behind them, the boatman lit another cigarette and continued punting in silence.

'Well,' said Siobhan, tipping ash thoughtfully overboard, 'it's very important to God that we have free will.'

He digested this.

'It's one of the most important things to Him. We have been born, and we have been given the freedom to do what we want. Now what He wants us to do is make the decision to follow Him, to love Him and to do his works. But this means we have to be *free* to make this decision; we have to have choice. If He forces us to love him then He hasn't achieved anything. And we haven't achieved anything either. So if we accept we have free will, then it means that the terrorists had free will to do what they wanted on September 11th.'

'But the terrorists believed that was what God wanted them to do,' he objected.

'Well,' she said, frowning, 'now you're shifting the goal posts. You were saying how can God allow such a thing, and I'm explaining why; this has got nothing to do with what the terrorists thought or didn't think. Yes, the terrorists believed that God wanted them to do that. Maybe they're right, I don't know, we're not in a position to say whether He did or didn't. Of course, you and I think He didn't; and they think He did. Neither of us can say what God did or didn't want; we just have an opinion, a belief, and those responsible for September 11th had a belief too.'

He nodded, surprised by her even-handedness. He expected her to dismiss them out of hand as wrong.

'Either way,' she continued, 'the important thing is that we have free will and the terrorists do as well. Neither point you've made means that there *isn't* a God; nor does it mean He's not a merciful God.'

He raised his eyebrows, effectively silenced. She smiled. 'I didn't think I'd be able to say it as clearly as that.' It was as if she had executed a particularly effective and unexpected move at chess. She breathed deeply.

'But he could have stepped in and stopped it,' he objected.

She nodded. 'Yes, He could. But that would have taken away a major and fundamental part of what it means to be human.'

He dragged slowly on his cigarette, and flicked the butt into the water. It fizzed and glowed orange, and disappeared. He nodded, carefully preparing his next move. 'What's the point in prayer then?'

'What do you mean?'

'Well, for example, if everyone has free will, then there's no point in praying for, say, a child who has been abducted. Because if the person who has abducted her is going to murder her, he has the free will to do that. So praying to God isn't going to stop it, because he wants that murderer to have free will.'

'But equally, *we* have the free will to pray. And if you're praying before he's murdered her, the murderer still has the free will to change his mind and not be a murderer. Perhaps if we pray hard enough for him to change his mind, he might change his mind.'

He frowned, marginally confused; wondering whether he was confused, or whether he just disagreed. 'But God won't make him change his mind, because God wants him to have free will. It doesn't matter whether the will is to murder, or whether the will is to change your mind.'

'Eh?'

'If free will can be influenced by God, it isn't free will,' he said carefully. 'If God's changing your mind for you, because lots of people have been praying to him and asking him to, you don't have the free will to do your own thing. Why would he step in and change the murderer's mind, if he wants the murderer to have free will? And if the murderer has free will, there's no point in praying for the child.'

They floated gently past trees on the bank and neared the botanical gardens. The boatman drew another cigarette from the packet with his teeth.

'You're missing the point,' she said.

'Am I?'

'You like asking impossible questions, don't you?' she said.

'Why isn't phonetic spelt with an 'f'? Why is there only one monopolies commission? Why is pronunciation pronounced pronunciation, why isn't it pronounced pronounciation? Who first coined the phrase 'to coin a phrase'? Why does monosyllabic have so many – '

She put her hands over her ears and giggled. 'Okay, stop, stop! All right, I didn't explain it very well.' She looked at him and pursed her lips. 'I'm not the best person to talk to, I'm not an expert. It's like playing chess with you; you know you can always catch me out. Do I have to take my top off?'

He smirked at her. The boatman coughed on his cigarette. Siobhan looked up at him, unembarrassed. 'Oh, hello,' she said, holding her hand up to shade her eyes. 'I'd forgotten you were there.'

The boat floated on in silence and they looked around. Siobhan looked down over the side of the boat and watched the greenish black water gently rippling, the sparkles of water on the surface like the light on the diamond in her ring.

'Doesn't mean I'm wrong though,' she said softly.

'No, no,' he said, 'I know. I just like a good argument.'

'No you don't.'

'Yes I do.'

'Are there any art galleries in Oxford?' she asked after a while. 'You know, in your *poncey* bit of Oxford.'

'Oh yeah, of course there are.' He looked at his watch. 'But four o'clock on a Sunday... they'll be closing by now.'

They lapsed into silence again. When we spend time together, he thought, do we do enough things? We just wander around... what does she spend her time thinking?

'So,' he said delicately, 'you know... if you are... if you are...?' She looked at him blankly, waiting for him to finish his sentence. 'Then...' he continued slowly, rotating his hand in a circle, 'then you'll definitely – I mean you know what you would do. You would definitely... keep it?'

'Oh yes, of course.' She looked at him with her wide-open blue eyes. 'I would never have an abortion, never. Not even if it completely ruined my life. I mean I don't think it *will* completely ruin my life, you know. I'm getting used to the idea, I'm quite okay with it really. Of course mum and dad will hit the roof.' She shrugged. 'Can't be helped. And we're both fine with it, Paul will come and live me in Edinburgh and get a job or... whatever, and I'll finish my degree and I'll get a bit of extra time because I'll have a kid, so that'll be good, and – well, everything will be okay.'

He nodded slowly. This was characteristic of the old Siobhan. As she had got it into her head that everything would be okay, she did not consider the possibility that it might not be okay. What did Paul think; was he really okay about it? Would it be as easy for him to get a job as Siobhan seemed to think? What kind of job would he be able to get; would it be one that could provide for three people?

Nickolas could imagine him saying to her, 'What are we going to *do*,' openly, not suggesting anything, waiting to see what she would say – the kind of way Nickolas used to deal with her, worrying that she would explode if he said what *he* thought. And he could see Siobhan shrugging and saying, 'you can move to Edinburgh and get a job.'

And that would be that, and Paul would nod slowly the way Nickolas used to, and digest this. That would be that for Siobhan too; she would move on to think about something else and not worry about it any more. The problem would be solved.

'So what does Paul think about this?' he asked.

'Oh yeah, he's fine about it.' She looked away from him and watched the swans swimming past, their necks bobbing. Nickolas is like a swan, she thought. Apparently he's very cool and calm, and never shows emotions and never lets you know what he's thinking. But you know that behind that calm exterior his brain is paddling away like fury, just below the surface of the water, moving much more quickly than you would expect. He thinks I don't think about things, but I do. And he thinks I've drifted off now, that I'm not thinking about what he's thinking; but I am. And we're both thinking about the other, but we don't really know what the other's thinking. She nodded thoughtfully.

She looked at the water. When she picked it up in the palm of her hand it was completely translucent, but when she dropped it back into the river, it was black and opaque.

He watched her looking at the water. So she's come off the pill, he thought; and then she has 'forgotten' and had sex without condoms; was she subconsciously *trying* to have a baby? What was Paul playing at; he must have *known* what he could be letting himself in for.

Or had she not told him she had come off the pill? She must have done, surely? Why's she getting married anyway; we know she'll have an affair.

And it will probably be with me, he thought, with an equal mixture of fear and hope. Her face was open and blank, a smile playing round the corners of her mouth, as if she could tell what he was thinking.

Or perhaps we don't know. Perhaps he doesn't mind anyway. But if he doesn't mind, why are they getting married, why not just go out with each other? He put his hand in the water and stared at the transparent liquid making the palm of his hand look green.

VI

They walked into the centre. Deep in the recesses of a decaying, must-ridden bookshop, she stuck her head above a precarious parapet of books balanced on the edge of a shelf and frowned at him.

'This is all crap,' she declared.

'I know,' he said. 'Abe.com is the place to buy books. That's where I get all mine. Everything here is what no one wants, at prices that no one would pay. I mean look at this.'

He picked up a very elderly orange Penguin copy of *Kangaroo* by Lawrence. It was dog-eared, had coffee spilt over it, and when he flicked through it the pages were so brown, even in the text block, that it would give you a headache trying to read it. It smelt like his grandmother's house. He showed it to Siobhan. When she looked inside, it was marked up at £6.

'Six pounds?' she declared in utter disbelief, her voice echoing round the shop. Six pounds, the scandalised shelves muttered to themselves. Not only did it smell like his grandmother, he could see her folding her arms in disgust and saying the words, describing what you could get for six pounds in her day.

Nickolas pointed to the scrawled pencillings below the price. ' "First Penguin edition, 1950." '

She shrugged. 'So?'

'Well,' he said apologetically, unsure exactly why he was apologising, considering that it wasn't his fault, 'early Penguin editions are quite collectable now. Apparently.'

'What, in this state,' she said, critically holding the book up by one corner as if it had been passed by an animal after a disagreeable meal.

He raised his eyebrows in an attitude of regret. 'Well I know,' he said, 'this is what I mean... everything's overpriced...'

'I mean so it's not even like *the* first edition,' she said, 'which okay, I understand, would probably be worth something whatever the condition. It's just the first *Penguin* edition. Wow, big *deal*. I mean,' she said, and as she raised her voice he had a flashback of standing outside the kiosk in the botanical gardens – the bookshop was small and very quiet – 'this is just a second-hand book, you wouldn't *collect* this, you'd only buy it to read it.' She proceeded to demolish it even further. 'You can't even do that, it's in such rubbish condition. Spend a pound more in Waterstones, and you can buy a nice clean new copy with a decent introduction and notes.'

He nodded silently. Words were no use any longer.

'And what's more,' she said, delivering the killer blow, 'it's shit.'

'Is it?'

She waved the unfortunate book about so that its spine started to detach from the covers. 'Yes,' she said, 'have you *read* it?'

He shook his head.

She dropped it back in the bookcase where it lay on its spine like a dying insect, its pages slowly falling open like legs waving helplessly in the disinterested breeze.

In another bookshop, once Siobhan had calmed down, she found a book called *Sex in Literature*. 'This looks quite good,' she said. It was a rather dull looking plain green hardbacked book, published in about 1970, written by someone he had never heard of. He expected it to be about subdued eroticism in Austen, or a dry analysis of censored sections in early editions of Thomas Hardy; pig's pizzles and the like. But when he flicked through it, it had chapter headings like 'Dildo' and 'The Masturbatory Instinct'.

'I might have to read this,' he murmured, as she paid at the door and they left.

He led her down a side alley with a high metal gate in it, and along a narrow path.

'Where are we going?' she said suspiciously. 'Where are you taking me?'

They emerged along the side of Christchurch and walked along the gravel path. She looked in admiration at the red and green creeper smothering the sides of the buildings; the yellow, crumbly stone; the trees dotted at occasional intervals throughout the sprawling, rambling park.

'Autumn's fantastic isn't it,' she said. 'The colours are so amazing.' It had been hot all day, but now it was getting late in the afternoon it rapidly became cold; they could sense September turning into October as they walked.

Siobhan closed her eyes and listened, almost in ecstasy, to the sound of the bright yellow gravel crunching underneath her feet. She felt the sharp chill of cold autumn air on her face, and breathed in, and took huge mouthfuls of smoky, crisp air into her lungs; then opened her eyes and looked at the greens and browns around her. A shoal of leaves swept across the grass in a sudden breeze. She could feel her nose and ears going red.

'You know,' she said, 'it's absolutely amazing being alive, isn't it?'

He nodded; it was as if he had never thought of it before, how incredible it was just existing, being able to see and experience things. He felt a sense of connection between them that transcended merely walking along together on a path. It was as if this moment would always exist.

'It's just so... amazing.'

He squeezed her hand, and she held onto him tightly. 'Yes,' he said quietly, 'it really is amazing.' They walked along together.

'I mean,' she said, 'when you think about it, it's ridiculous that *we're* not getting married. There was a time when I thought we would, you know.'

'Why do you think we didn't then?' Nickolas said. He said this without even working out his own thoughts on it; he just wanted to see what she would say.

'What, apart from Elaine you mean?'

'Er – yeah, apart from Elaine. There isn't an Elaine now.'

'I know. Well – ' she said, 'I suppose, if I could have met someone like you, but less irritating, it would have been great.'

He nodded.

'I mean who knows, I could meet someone now who's like you but less irritating. Who knows. Anything could happen.'

Siobhan's view was, why worry about it now. She was good at not being rhetorical; she didn't have the patience for it, which was probably why she found him irritating, because he was always being rhetorical. And now there wasn't an Elaine; if she were meeting him now…

But it was too late now. She was engaged. And pregnant.

Siobhan was thinking, how annoying it is, I have, in effect, just met someone who's like him but less irritating. Because now, *he* is less irritating. And there's no Elaine. But it's too late. It's always too late.

They reached the end of the gardens, walked round the corner and saw the imposing tower of Christchurch.

'So is this the college you went to then?'

'Yes.'

'You would go for the one with the big phallic tower, wouldn't you; you can't go for one of the smaller, less portentous colleges.'

'Do you mean pretentious?'

'No, I know what I mean.'

'It's called Tom Tower.'

'Is it.'

They walked past the gates and peered inside at the square of green and the rooms beyond.

'So have the panic attacks gone?' she asked. They were heading back into town. Around them, the last tourists of the summer swarmed into Waterstones and Debenhams.

He hesitated before he replied. 'No. They're not as bad as they were though.' He tried to look optimistic when her face fell. She was hoping he was better. He *seemed* better; he seemed so much more laid back today. She also wished that she could convince him that everything would be okay, so that he could stop fearing things so much, stop fearing the obliteration that he always used to bang on about. Siobhan could never comprehend what was so terrifying; but then of course she knew that God existed.

It was one of the things that had stopped their relationship working; he knew that she knew that it was one of the things that had driven him back to Elaine. Elaine was better at dealing with it; when he was in the troughs of depression she knew how to help him out. Siobhan just got frustrated, or didn't comprehend what was going on.

Or he had thought that she did not comprehend what was going on; now, he realised, she did. To Nickolas she had seemed insensitive or insufficiently interested; but it was just that she couldn't find the words to explain things to him. She didn't know what to say and they ended up going round and round in circles, and then she would change the subject. He saw this as impatience.

'I'm in control of them,' he said, 'they only happen one or two nights a week instead of, you know – all the time.'

'Yes.' She paused, remembering. 'So,' she said, 'are you still on Prozac, or whatever it was?'

He smiled. 'It's not Prozac. But yes, I'm still on them.'

'I thought you were going to try to come off them.'

'I went through a phase a while after we broke up where it got worse, a lot worse, so I went back to him and he's put me on three a night now instead of two. I think that's the maximum.'

'I don't think that's very, er... I mean you can't go on like that *forever*, can you?'

He winced. 'Well, they work, that's the point. And they're not addictive.'

She shrugged. He could tell she didn't believe him; she thought he was trying to convince himself.

'What is this fear anyway, I mean how does it manifest itself?'

Nickolas looked around. Across the road, a man pushed a glass door and went into a poster shop. A child cycled along an alleyway, ringing his bell, the wheels bouncing on the yellow gravel. A girl in a long black coat and black boots pushed her scarf over her shoulder and unlocked her car. The orange indicators flashed twice. Ahead of him, fast-moving clouds crossed the bright blue wedge of sky visible between buildings. The leaves rustled gently in the breeze.

'Well,' he said, 'it's an abstract, simple fear of not existing any more. Well, it's not abstract, it's very real. The fear of obliteration. I've got so much I want to do...'

'Well, you will be able to do everything. You've got... well, fifty or sixty years.'

He bit the skin inside his cheek. 'It sounds,' he said as they walked past the bookshops and cafés again, 'I don't know, daft or selfish or something... but sixty years isn't really enough.' She smiled at him, then quickly removed the smile as she saw the look of concentration on his face.

'It's no time at all compared to eternity of non-existen – ' he broke off, shivering, looking as if he had hiccupped painfully. A twinge of angst went through him.

'Anyway,' he said, in a different tone of voice, holding his palm in front of his face as if to shield himself from the idea, 'it's an existentialist thing – the total, consuming horror of not being any more.'

'But it's so far away,' she said, tugging at his arm.

'It doesn't really matter, because this is *everything* that we're talking about.' He looked at her uncomfortably, as if apologetic for sounding ungrateful.

Conversations with Magic Stones

In the yellow light of late afternoon he looked older. There were lines on his face and his skin seemed grey and tired. 'I think if I knew I was going to live to be 200,' he said, and she was struck by the melodic sound of his voice, lifting above the rhythmical crunch of stones under their feet, 'I would still have the same shuddering horror and terror. It's the fact that it's *going to happen*, there's no escaping it, that's the awful thing.' He glanced at her. 'Not even "probably" will happen, "might not" happen, "there's always a chance it won't" happen. It's one hundred per cent.'

She stared at the stone on her ring, and turned it from side to side, and watched it glittering and glowing. 'Well, yes, it is going to happen,' she murmured. 'Nothing you can do about it.'

'That doesn't help,' he said, biting his tongue.

She shook her head, thinking about something, and the stone glinted and her eyes glazed and the stone became misty, translucent, and a cloud appeared in front of her eyes. She looked up at Nickolas and blinked.

'You just have to...' she said, and trailed off. 'I can't explain it.' She was cross with herself. 'I want to explain it...'

He reached out and touched her hand. The connection vibrated through both of them. They both understood something, even if they weren't sure exactly what it was they understood, and even if one of them understood something slightly different from the other.

'*Wow* – '

Nickolas looked round. Siobhan had turned to watch a man in a thick winter coat, buttoned up to the neck, walking past with his shoulders hunched. He looked to Nickolas like a professor. He had grey hair pushed back from his receding forehead and thick, dark eyebrows.

'For a minute I thought that was Keith.'

'Who's Keith?'

She grinned at him. 'Keith's the oldest person I've... you know. He's 46.'

'You are a very naughty girl.'

She grinned. 'I know. He's really sexy though, really distinguished looking, which makes people look really powerful and horny, don't you think?'

'Do you think I'll be that sexy when I'm 46?' he asked. He said it coyly, deliberately to get a reaction from her. The response was not quite what he expected. She snorted, and gazed at him with wide eyes. 'I *hope* so,' she said emphatically. 'I mean I'll be in my... what, *mid-thirties*... that just seems an *age* away... You *better* be that sexy.' She nodded to herself. 'We'll have to have an affair,' she said decisively.

He said nothing for a while then spoke almost irritably. 'I don't see why you're getting married when you say things like that.' They were walking quickly now, not really noticing the people and the shops; the momentum of the conversation carried them along.

She raised her eyebrows. 'What do you mean?'

'Well – isn't it supposed to be about forsaking all others, isn't that the whole point of marriage?'

'Yeah, yeah, I know.' She wriggled uncomfortably. 'I do mean it, well part of me does.' She concentrated on the square paving stones as they walked. 'Oh, I don't know, whatever – do we have to talk about this now?' She folded her arms as they reached the bridge, and stopped halfway across it. They looked down into the water.

'Is he okay with you coming out with me today?'

'Yeah, of course he is.' She looked him in the eye with pale,

sincere blue eyes. 'I know I don't want to sleep with anyone else ever again.'
He listened to the water rushing underneath them.
'I do know that, I know it when I think it through. I mean I know I say flippant things to you.'
He nodded.
'I told him, I was blunt, I said if I wanted to seduce you, if I wanted to *be* with you, I probably could be.'
He nodded again, still not saying anything, not giving anything away by his expression, just assimilating what she was saying. He noticed the 'probably'.
'And I told him, I'm *not* doing that, I want to be with him, the very fact of how I'm behaving should prove to him how I want things to be. But,' she said, tugging at his arm and looking up at him, 'that doesn't mean I don't want to spend the day with you, or that I don't want to do things with you.'
Why do we keep returning to this bridge, he wondered, why do we always seem to end up standing here and looking down at the river and the botanical gardens? They started walking again, crossed between the steady stream of traffic and looked down past the heavy overhanging trees towards where the boats were moored. Every few moments a punt emerged from the still backwater and floated down the river, like a new child being born.
'So anyway,' she was saying, 'it's going to be fantastic, I'm going to move to Edinburgh, wa-hey, away from Boringland, and get a job teaching, Paul will come with me and everything will be great. How's your job going, by the way?'
'Oh well... all right I suppose.' He was nearly ten years older than her, he thought; she was getting organised and mapping her life out and getting married and having a baby; and his life wasn't going anywhere and everything was the same as it had been when he had left Oxford.

'So yeah anyway,' she said, as they walked along the Cowley Road again, 'I really want you to be involved. I want you to be Godfather to my child.'

He shrugged. 'I'd love to. But why bring God into it?'

She laughed, frowned, then went rapidly on to something else. 'And,' she said, 'obviously I want you to be at the wedding, you know. And when I've moved up to Edinburgh, I still want you to come and see me, and have great days like we used to. Like we still do. Like today.' She pushed her arm through his and walked along with her head on his shoulder.

VII

They went to a pub which according to Siobhan was called the Queen's Head. But when they got there it was covered in orange neon and a bright sign declared it was the Cap and Ferret. Nickolas looked up at it dubiously.

Siobhan was standing with her mouth open. 'What's happened here,' she said quietly, disbelievingly. 'This used to be the nicest pub around here.'

'Perhaps it's still okay once you get inside,' said Nickolas, in a rare moment of optimism. He didn't sound convinced.

Siobhan's immediate instinct was to carry along the road and find another pub. They walked for a hundred yards or so and then she stopped. He bumped into her. 'No,' she said decisively, 'we must go in, and see what it's like, and lay the ghost to rest. Otherwise I'll be thinking about it all evening. We have to go and see.'

'Okay,' said Nickolas. 'I'm happy whatever.'

He followed her across the road. It was one of the reasons their friendship had survived, he thought, that he was happy whatever. Things were usually on Siobhan's terms and if Nickolas had not been the sort of person to be happy whatever, no matter how erratic she might seem, then she would get irritable and spiky.

Siobhan, for her part, knew that she was hard work and volatile. She also knew that people thought she didn't realise what she was like; but she knew perfectly well. One of the things she liked most about Nickolas – especially the new, calmer Nickolas who she was now spending the day with – was that he would always put up with her suggestions, even when she knew they might not be what he wanted to do. He had the grace to accept what she said without arguing for the sake of it, or trying to assert himself, or any of that rubbish.

She knew that he knew that she knew that she was a bit prickly, and she admired the fact that he was above arguing with her, and that his way of dealing with it was to go along with it and let her think she had won. In many ways, she thought, we understand each other better than we ever say to each other. She wondered whether or not to tell him this.

He followed her into the pub. Inside, it had evidently once been a traditional, oak panelled pub, dark and gloomy, with several small lounge bars or public bars, and wooden doors with little brass signs. Now, it had been stripped out, the bars had been knocked together and everything was brightly lit. Nickolas made to go to the bar but Siobhan skipped ahead of him. 'You find a table,' she said. 'Not that one with the, like, *elephant shit* behind it.'

When he looked, he saw what she meant; there was a large painting behind one of the tables with an abstract design made up of thick, blobby brown paint, raised several inches up from the surface of the canvas. It made him smile. He sat at an adjoining table.

It was only five-thirty, and the pub looked like the kind of place that would become extremely busy and noisy at about half past eight. They sat at one of the vast, scrubbed pine benches. The décor was plain and functional; olive green paint, rapidly and thinly applied to wooden slats, like decking that had been uprooted and stuck onto the walls. The plaster had then been left rough and unpainted above. The paint was already starting to chip away to the walls underneath in places where the chairs or doors had knocked against it.

Siobhan came back with a bottle of white wine, condensation running gleamingly down its sides. Nickolas had a strong and vivid picture of her tongue running the length of his penis, leaving a shining trail of saliva that was just like the glistening liquid on the neck of the bottle. When she ran her hand across the bottle, the steamy, opaque green film disappeared and the wine, bubbling slightly from being disturbed, was visible within. Siobhan poured two glasses. Nickolas, closing his eyes, listened to the glugging, almost metallic sounding wine filling up the glass, the pitch getting higher and higher until the music disappeared above the scale of hearing.

He opened his eyes and looked at Siobhan.

'Oh,' he murmured, looking at the glasses, 'how am I supposed to drink that?' The glasses were filled to the brim.

Siobhan grinned. 'That's the challenge. To drink it without spilling a drop.'

They both slowly picked their glasses up. Nickolas stared at the top of the glass, willing the wine to stay inside. It wobbled, and looked as if it should tip over the brim, but as he brought it to his mouth it stayed in the glass. It appeared to have a kind of skin on it, that you could tip very very slightly to one side. Although he expected it to splash over the edge, it remained where it was. Nickolas sipped slowly and carefully until he had a full mouthful, then he felt safe to move his mouth away and put the glass down. He held the liquid in his cheeks for a moment, looked at Siobhan, and swallowed.

Meanwhile Siobhan lifted her glass carefully to her mouth, then at the point where she was about to push her lips forward to drink without making any real contact with the glass, her arm reached a critical height/balance/weight interface and her hand started shaking. The wine spilt on the table, Siobhan giggled and put the glass down, then she used her arm to wipe the wine across the table. It did not absorb into the wood; it lay in small globules and puddles, like water on a waxed surface.

The tiny hairs on Siobhan's arm were matted and sticky with wine. Looking at Nickolas and not taking her eyes off him for a moment, Siobhan put her tongue out to its full length and ran it up and down her arm.

The room swam slightly; olive green waves lapped up and down against a whitewashed building on their shore.

Nickolas smiled at Siobhan. She smiled back at him. He looked down at his glass. 'Have I drunk that already?' he said, frowning in consternation.

She grinned. 'Yes,' she said, rapidly tipping more wine into his glass. The wine filled up like an inverted, large rolling wave, as she tried to tip it more quickly than the glass could easily accommodate it.

He drank another long mouthful of wine. She watched him. Yes, she thought, yes. I really want to go out with him now. Shit.

She shrugged. From a lazy corner of an eye he noticed her

and wondered what she was shrugging about, then forgot about it and stared blindly around the bar.

Siobhan lit up another cigarette, closing her eyes against the smoke that curled around her, as they were in a corner of the bar with no breeze. Oh yeah, she thought, baby. She shrugged again. Ah well. I'm sure it will cope. I'll give up when it's proved definite.

He opened his eyes. 'I really don't think you should be smoking.'

'I know, you're right. But we still don't *know*, do we?'

He shook his head, not wanting to argue. We do know, he thought, and you know it too. But if it's confirmed tomorrow, then she's probably right, today's cigarettes don't make much difference if it's survived up to today. He knew that she would be sincere and give up drinking and smoking when she believed it was true. So he did not press her.

She rested her hand over his hand. He looked at the contrast, her pale white hands and dark red nails alternating with his brown, hairy hands and rough chipped nails. She pushed her fingers between the spaces in his fingers and pressed her flesh into his. She looked up at him. 'I want you in my mouth,' she murmured.

He looked away and frowned. 'You're playing with me now,' he said. He looked back at her and concentrated on her eyes. 'You know you can wrap me round your finger.'

'I know,' she said, as she looked at the entwined fingers; he's used the term 'wrapped round your finger', she thought, because it's our fingers he's been looking at; but he doesn't realise his brain has made the connection. 'But,' she said, 'I'm just imagining running my tongue up and down all over you.' She glanced up at him and did not blink.

He leant forward and kissed her on the lips. Her tongue

snaked into his mouth before he pulled away again. 'You're such a tease,' he said. He sat back and looked around the pub. 'I shall have to find someone like you who isn't getting married,' he said.

'Then you'll have to become gay or something,' she said, 'because there's no one like me.' She grinned at him. 'I'm extra special.'

'Hmm.' He drained another glass of wine.

'I mean you must have at least snogged a bloke.'

'What?' he said, wondering where that had come from. 'No,' he said innocently, 'nothing.'

'How boring. What, not even at college? I kissed lots of girls at college, but I only went to bed with one of them, which was a shame. You should definitely find out what it's like with a guy.'

'Oh, right. Yes, I suppose so. I'm not sure I would want anything, you know... *penetrative.*'

'No.'

'But,' he said, as his drunkenness ran away with him and he said he things he had not thought of before, or would not have thought of saying even if he had thought of them, 'the idea of giving someone a blow-job is interesting.'

She nodded.

'I want to do everything,' he said, and he didn't sound excited by the prospects and opportunities of life, he sounded sad. He looked down at the glass. 'Go everywhere,' he continued, 'experience everything you can experience. Sometimes I think I'm just running on a tenth of capacity; do you ever get that feeling?'

Someone walked past near to their table and glanced at them. Nickolas realised he was speaking loudly, and deliberately; it was as if his tongue was too large for his mouth.

She nodded again. 'And,' he continued, 'I feel capable of doing so much, and I just don't feel I get anywhere near what I could do with my life.'

'I know. I feel that I have lived,' she said thoughtfully. 'I have done everything I want to do. That's why I want to settle down and get married. You just need more things to happen to you. So going out with a guy would be amazing for you. And yeah...' she grinned at him, teasing again, wrapping her finger round the rapidly emptying wine bottle, 'blow-jobs are amazing.'

'Although,' he said, 'I think I might get a bit nervous when it came to the actual, you know, *moment.*'

'Oh well,' she said, rolling her eyes, 'join the rest of us. Welcome to what it's like to be a girl.' He nodded thoughtfully, as if she had said something wise.

She leant forward and bit his ear. 'But you always tasted fantastic.'

VIII

'What?' He must have had his eyes closed again. He tried to focus on her. She was leaning across the table towards him and her eyes were huge and blue in her head. He blinked; his head felt fuzzy. When he looked up at the huge clock behind her, he was utterly astonished to discover that it was only six o'clock. It felt like about ten. She was talking about something or other; he tried to work out what.

'Because,' she continued, 'it's not fair, you know, that you suffer like this. Why do you go through all this pain, you don't need to.'

He tried to put the glass carefully down on the table, but let go before it quite reached the surface. It wobbled about for a moment, making a ringing sound. 'Well,' he said, finding it laborious to explain, and forgetting that he already had, 'it's because of this terrible fear of not existing any more. Can't describe it more clearly than that.' He shrugged. 'I don't think we'll get anywhere by talking about it, but, that's the problem, anyway.'

She studied him closely; his eyes watered and he looked away into the middle distance. She noticed that behind him there was a crack in the wall. He did not say anything for a while. Eventually he spoke. 'It, you know, it just makes everything, it makes everything awful.'

'You mean it makes life seem pointless?'

'Well – no...' He sounded uncertain. 'I want to live, I want to stay living, that's the thing. So life isn't pointless, no. But if it comes to an end and we just – ' he waved his arms around – 'vaporise into nothing, it's just...' he looked at her unhappily. 'Losing consciousness... I can't cope with it, that's all.' He forgot where the sentence had started, forgot what he wanted to say. He wanted to describe how incoherent he felt about things, but didn't seem able to.

She put her arms around him and hugged him close to her. 'Don't worry,' she said. 'You mustn't worry. There is a God, you know.'

He shook his head slowly.

'Honestly, there is. You must believe that. There is hope, and you will be born again, you will.'

He looked up at her, longing to believe her and not able to.

'Where the hell's that gone?' They frowned at the empty bottle. 'They don't last long, do they?' Nickolas went to the bar and bought another one. He sat down with it heavily. There was something incongruous about the fact that the new bottle was full, and the old bottle was empty, but both labels were exactly the same. They glanced back and forth between each bottle, both thinking the same thing.

Siobhan looked at him, wanting to help him, frightened that

she couldn't, supremely confident that he was worrying about nothing, wishing that she could communicate to him the fact that everything was going to be okay, willing her consciousness to pour into him and solve things for him. She clutched onto his hand, feeling the energy pulse from her into him; she hoped that by a kind of osmosis she could make him realise.

At the table next to them was a nervous man, not making any attempt to conceal the fact that he was looking at a girl at another table. Nickolas watched him, mirrored in the wall that slanted above him. The girl got up and went to the bar; the man, looking more nervous than ever, smiled at her. She did not respond.

Nickolas saw something of himself in the man. He seemed normal and reasonably intelligent, and not actually bad-looking. But he knew that he would never, ever get anywhere with the girl. He simply did not have the right kind of charm; the intangible but instantly recognisable ability to achieve success. Even if the girl was attracted, Nickolas knew she would never say yes to him.

He turned back to Siobhan. 'I just don't believe it,' he said. 'I really wish I could believe it's true.'

'It is true. It is true.'

'I'd like to, I… I *used* to…'

'Do you totally, totally not then? You think it's all rubbish?'

He swallowed. 'I can consider it. I just don't believe it. I try to have an open mind. There's always a small amount of doubt.'

'Is there?' she said hopefully, willing him to concentrate on this doubt.

He shrugged. 'You can't prove that there isn't a God. Because there will always be 'the unknown.' You can prove there *is* a God, if you find evidence. That's the advantage you have, by definition. That's where the hope lies. But I don't see any evidence for it. And lack of evidence, to anyone non-religious, is as good as proof that there isn't a God.'

'But you have doubt.'

He pulled a face, and eventually shook his head. 'I don't believe it,' he said disconsolately. 'I'm 99% convinced there's no God.'

'Why?'

'There's no logic to it.'

'It doesn't have anything to do with logic.' She smiled. 'You're so bogged down with logic and rationality, and being so *intelligent*, and all the rest of it. Is it rational that we're here at all?'

'Eh?'

'Well, in your logical, rational universe, if there's no God and there is only logic, why is there anything material at all? Why is there a universe, why is there existence instead of non-existence?'

'I'm not with you.'

She was patient. 'Surely the most rational state for the universe to be in would be – that there's nothing at all. The most normal, *logical* state of affairs would be for there to be no sound, no light. No *matter*.'

He shook his head. 'The universe was created by accident,' he said, 'the big bang was just an accidental explosion of chemicals combusting.'

'But how did those chemicals come into existence? How can there be chemicals? How can there be energy, light, how can there *be* anything at all?'

He shrugged. 'Accident. That's all.'

'But *why?* What caused the accident? If I knock over a glass, it's an accident, but caused by me. Accidents don't just happen by themselves; there has to be a cause. The glass, the wine, the chair and the momentum all have to exist already to make an 'accident' occur. Nothing can just come into being without a cause, and however you want to look at it, that cause is God.'

He shook his head. 'We're back to the old problem of who created God.'

She sighed.

'You're saying there had to be a God to create the universe, so I say who created God.'

'No one created God.'

'Well if you can believe God just 'came into being', why can't you accept the universe 'came into being'? That way, you can explain things just as effectively, without having to invoke a supernatural being. Occam's razor.' He slurred on the unfamiliar words and shook his head sadly. Into his mind came the phrase 'Ozzam's raker'. He shook his head. 'I don't buy any of it.'

'You should do. You really should do.' She rubbed his shoulder. She wanted to take him into her arms and hug him until he believed her. She knew God wanted her to communicate his belief to him by the osmosis she had thought of earlier on, for want of a better word, if there was no way of making him listen to the words.

'Why?' he said innocently, hopelessly.

'Because it's true,' she answered simply.

He was tearful. She kissed his cheek and tasted the salt. 'Jesus loves you,' she said softly, looking into his eyes. 'How can I make you realise how sincere I am?' Nickolas opened his mouth to speak, but she put her finger against his lips. 'I'm not giving you an evangelical hard sell,' she whispered. 'He really does. Jesus loves you, he thinks you're great. You're the man for him.'

He stared down at the empty glass of wine. From the way she was talking, it sounded almost – he stopped himself, and shook his head, and prevented himself from thinking what he was thinking.

Conversations with Magic Stones

Her voice continued; soft, coaxing, persuading.

On the next table, the man was talking to the girl. Nickolas couldn't hear everything he said to her, but large sections of his words were audible, like chunks of iceberg floating past him in the slow-moving sludge of endless, monotonous conversation that surrounded him.

'I'm a writer,' the man was saying, 'and I'm after characters, and I wondered if I could spend the day with you?'

The girl's response was indistinct, but the answer was not yes. Her voice was less penetrating than his. The man smiled nervously and persisted. Someone dropped a plate behind the bar and Nickolas missed the start of the sentence.

'...can tell that, it's very evident, and I think if I just spent an afternoon with you... someone along with you if you like, I'm not a weirdo, I'm not going to... and chop you up into little bits... thought you looked really interesting... find out what you do for the day, what goes on in your life... would get a really good character from it.'

Nickolas's face was sinking into his hand. He noticed he had a cigarette between his fingers, but did not remember Siobhan giving it to him or lighting it. He lifted his head off the hand, pulled the cigarette round towards his mouth and breathed in a mouthful.

Siobhan was murmuring in his ear. 'Just believe me, don't worry about your own doubt. It *is* true, and Jesus loves you. He loves you, he loves you...' she gently curled his hair in her fingers. She smiled her broad, blissful smile, and pressed her nose up against his hair. He smelt her breath in his face, and she spoke so closely into his ear that his skin tingled and the hairs on his spine stood up.

'He truly does,' she whispered, holding his head and rubbing his hair. 'He wants you for himself...'

At the next table, the girl was nodding and the man was nodding back. She wrote something down on a piece of paper for him, delicately pushing her hair behind her ear as she did so. She got up and pulled her skirt down to her knees, then grinned at the man and walked away. She left the pub. The man drained his glass and left the pub by a different door.

Nickolas's head nodded into his lap. Siobhan took the glass of wine from his hand, where it had been held at such a severe angle that drops of wine were spilling onto his trousers and making small round stains like blood.

He could see the room spinning, like when you have spent a week on a boat and, back on dry land, rooms move. Thoughts swam in his head. It can't be true, he was thinking. What are the chances of it being true? It's not, I know it's not. Who was more likely to be right? Someone who was rational, logical and rigorously intellectual? Or someone like her, who's wonderful and fantastic, but ultimately a space – here he hiccupped – cadet.

Siobhan lifted him up and hauled him from the pub. 'Got to show you the station,' he said carefully. 'Got to get you to the station.'

'I can remember the way back to the station,' she said, 'I'll guide you.' She put her arm round him and led him across the wide, open roundabout that led to the bridge, remembering for some of the journey to watch out for cars.

'You're different,' he mumbled. 'You've calmed down, you're not the way you were. I love being with you now. I love the person – *icth* – I love you,' he said, frowning.

They loped away towards the bridge, staggering from time to time. A driver, thinking they were going to stumble in front of him, screeched to a halt and gave an annoyed beep when they didn't.

IX

They crossed the bridge, sobered slightly by the fresh air and walking separately now in an approximation of a straight line. Their legs ached; it was the fourth time they had crossed the bridge that day.

She glanced up at him and quickly, matter-of-factly, bit him on the neck, lightly this time. She looked across the road and saw the cars passing by in the darkness, their headlights casting beams of light on the road that bent towards each other because of the curve of the bridge.

She ran ahead, crossed the road in a tight space between cars and in one deft movement, pulled her top off. She ran around with the top held high above her head, letting it flutter like a flag in the breeze. Her bra gleamed white and shiny in the dull blue light. Cars honked their horns enthusiastically as they drove past. An old Fiesta slowed to a halt, the windows were energetically wound down and two young men put their heads out of the windows and whistled.

Siobhan danced in a carefree way, with all the time in the world. In a gap between the traffic Nickolas hastily ran across the road to her side of the bridge. As he did so, Siobhan removed her bra and tossed it over the edge. It fell into the black water and disappeared, re-emerging a moment later and floating downstream like a pair of luminous buoys.

They looked down at the botanical gardens and remembered the afternoon spent gently touching the leaves of plants and wondering what things were called. Siobhan closed her eyes and leant her hands against the cool, crumbly stone. She gripped at the fabric of the bridge with her fingertips. Small flakes of stone came away under her fingernails like crumbs of cake. She dug her nails in, lifted her feet up and stared down into the black water.

Nickolas put his arm round her, shielding her. Slowly she opened her eyes again, blinked, and looked round to where her top had fallen, at some point, to the kerb of the road. She picked it up, her breasts lit up for a moment by the headlights of another passing car, which beeped its horn furiously. The top was crumpled and dirty but she pulled it on and Nickolas brushed it down.

'I needed to do that,' she murmured. They walked slowly to the other side of the bridge. Nickolas glanced back for a moment at the gardens. On the other side of the bridge, the unattended punts bobbed quietly in the dark, unnoticed water.

The train was nearly an hour late. As they sat on the platform waiting for it, they realised how hungry they were. It was nearly 10 o'clock and they had eaten nothing all day. Someone sat next to them on the uncomfortable seat and proceeded to chat Siobhan up, apparently oblivious to Nickolas's presence.

Siobhan mentioned during the conversation that she was engaged, pregnant and spending the evening with an ex-boyfriend, but none of these facts seemed to put him off. Above them, the huge digital clock ticked off the seconds with loud, ominous clicks, counting down to some indefinable moment in the future that never arrived.

The train sluggishly pulled in, brakes squealing intermittently as it feebly came to a halt. As the door hissed open and they stumbled aboard, Nickolas wondered why digital clocks on stations have audible ticks. Surely the whole point of a digital clock is that it doesn't need to tick – he shook his head and the thought vanished.

They managed to find two seats together and fell into them. Siobhan immediately dropped her head against the window and fell asleep, but as the train started up her head bounced against the window and she woke up. She looked up at him in confusion.

'Have we got there?' she asked.

'No, we're just leaving.'

'Just leaving *Oxford?*'

'Yes.'

'Oh.' She groaned, and rested her head again, then sprang back up and shifted around in the seat and snuggled up against his shoulder.

He woke her up at Reading and they changed trains. On the more spacious train back to Maidenhead, they sat opposite each other on the wide, smelly blue chairs, thick with the smell of smoke even though each carriage was supposedly no-smoking, and kept their heads away from the headrests which turned neatly from blue to greasy black. They looked aimlessly out of the window. Occasionally the odd light flashed past, but mostly they just stared at the incomprehensible tags and graffiti.

She glanced at him and as the train bumped and rolled, her head moved up and down slightly in time. She looked a little glazed.

'You've got a really sexy nose,' she said, looking at him intently.

Her voice sounded strange and unnatural, coming across the air to him after so long a silence.

'And this bit...' she leant forward and touched his chest, where a button of his shirt had come undone, '...is really sexy.' She rubbed her hand gently against the black hairs.

'This is what I've...'

He stopped. He wasn't sure what he had been intending to say. She wasn't really listening to him anyway; she was still studying his chest with great interest.

'This is what I've always found so odd about you,' he said eventually.

'What do you mean?' She sat back in her seat with a bump.

'Well, the way you are. And the things you do. To...' his mouth felt large and unwieldy again. 'To equate that with the Christian side of you. You're passionately religious...' – it sounded more like 'illijuzz,' – 'and yet, you're the way you are.'

She shrugged. 'You'll just have to get used to it, I'm afraid.'

'Yes,' he nodded thoughtfully, 'yes, you're right. I will. '

X

The next day she rang him at work. 'Hey,' she said, 'Listen to this. It's amazing.' He heard pages flickering.

When Salmacis beheld
His naked beauty, such strong pangs so ardently her held
That utterly she was astraught. And even as Phoebus' beams
Against a mirror pure and clear rebound with broken gleams,
Even so her eyes did sparkle fire.

And therewithal in all post haste she, having lightly thrown
Her garments off, flew to the pool and cast her thereinto,

And caught him fast between her arms for aught that he could do.
She held him still, and kissed him an hundred times and more.
And with her hands she touched his naked breast.
And now on this side, now on that, for all he did resist
And strove to wrest him from her grips, she clung unto him fast,
And wound about him like a snake, which snatched up in haste
And cast her tail about his wings displayed in the wind.

He put his feet up on the desk and listened to her. 'Wow,' he said. 'Is that really Ovid? I thought Ovid was really, you know... boring.'

'Nuh-huh,' she said dismissively. 'Oh, and I went to the doctor this morning,' she added, 'and I took my er – you know, *bottle* along.'

'Yes,' he said nervously.

Her voice was disembodied, unreal. It didn't sound like her. Something was bubbling up underneath her, something she wanted to say was about to spill out.

He felt his heart tug. Wires seemed to be stretched across his chest and were pulling him in different directions. He was pleased, he supposed, that she had decided that she was content with it. He was surprised at the pain he felt, surprised at the pangs of jealousy, envy; the sense of, well, this could be me having a child with her.

On the other hand, of course, he wouldn't want to have a child with her at the moment anyway. He frowned. He didn't want to marry her. Or did he? He felt confused, and although he identified the confusion, appreciated it. He did not expect to feel confused; he thought he knew how he felt about her.

Yesterday, his feelings had gone up and down and changed several times and now he didn't even know what he thought. But he was pleased she was okay with it; it would be awful, unimaginable, if she decided she really didn't want to be pregnant.

'Guess what?' she said.

He swallowed. Was it appropriate to say, 'Congratulations'? Or should he say –

'I'm not!' she exclaimed.

'What?'

'I'm not pregnant! Isn't that amazing?'

He said nothing for a moment. 'Yes, yes,' he quickly said; he was beaming broadly, so broadly that he found it difficult to speak, and it struck him as odd that his body wanted to smile so much, because she couldn't see it over the phone. A mixture of relief, combined with some other feeling he couldn't define, swept over him. His spine tingled, the base of his skull itched and prickled, and he experienced indescribable joy. He didn't know *why* he felt so happy; why such a sense of the rightness of being alive had come over him at that moment. It was such good news.

'I mean,' she was saying, 'what are the chances of that happening? I did a pregnancy test and it came out positive… and the chances against it being wrong are just, well… hardly any chance at all. Not even one per cent. Ninety-nine per cent impossible. And yet it's true!'

'I'm really pleased.'

'Me too. Just what are the chances!' she said again, her voice full of disbelief. He could hear the pattern of her voice shifting back and forth as she shook her head.

'Hey,' she said, and he lifted his eyebrows questioningly, again amazed at the way his body responded when he knew she couldn't see him. 'Listen to another bit,' she said, and he could hear the sharp, crackly intake of breath as she puffed on a cigarette. He listened to her voice, closed his eyes, and absorbed her gentle, soothing words.

Conversations with Magic Stones

Howbeit, she swam, and as she swam, my hand I softly laid
Upon her breast which quivered still. And while I touched the
same,
I sensibly did feel how all her body hard became:
And how the earth did overgrow her bulk. And as I spake,
New earth enclosed her swimming limbs, which by and by did take
Another shape, and grew into a mighty isle.

She stopped speaking and the phone clicked and she had gone.
Nickolas imagined the stone on her finger, glowing green.

holy and raw

past:

After I had cut his head off, I washed my hands over and over again and panicked about what I was going to do. Zoë, aged four, ran into the room. She suggested I stick his head back on with Sellotape. I laughed hollowly. I was going to have to do the whole print again; how I had managed to slice through his head was beyond me. I threw what was left of it on the floor.

I still had developing fluid on my hands. I washed them again but couldn't get rid of that tacky, sticky feeling. Like the sensation you get in dreams when something shadowy is slowly creeping up behind you, and you know you won't be able to shake it off.

I went into London again that week to photograph someone else. I hate London; it smells of diesel, chips and other people. I like the smell of other people when I'm choosing to smell them; I can't stand it when other peoples' odours are forced on me.

I went round to Andi's flat. The main door wasn't properly on its catch. I pushed my way in and walked up the stairs. I found her sprawled on top of a beautiful girl, screaming 'God!' at the top of her voice. 'Is it going all right?' I asked her conversationally.

She was roughly pushing two of her fingers into the girl's large, open mouth. 'I can't do this right!' gasped Andi, her face flushed red and the veins straining against her forehead. Her hands were covered with clay, and more clay smudged her nose.

'It looks all right to me,' I said. 'When's it meant to be finished by?'

'Five weeks,' she panted. 'It'll be all right. She's just messing me about a bit at the moment.' Andi wiped some of the clay off her nose and clambered down from the sculpture. 'Shall we go then?'

On the train I looked at the seats. They were mostly blue, but dark and dirty on the headrests from where greasy heads had been. I tried not to lean back in my seat. I concentrated on Andi's face instead. She was looking out of the window, an expression of mild interest on her face. I couldn't see what she was interested in. There was nothing out there but graffiti and plastic bags.

'What's up with you?' Andi asked me. I was sitting up stiffly in my seat.

'I'm trying not to lean back,' I replied. Andi pursed her lips then stared out of the window again. I looked outside and watched the pale blue reflection of Andi's face nod gently in time with the rhythm of the train.

We drew into the station. The train heaved to a halt, strange bits of it making groaning, sighing noises like a child being refused biscuits. Walking along I looked at parts of plastic wrapper, McDonald's cartons, bits of yellow stuff and old pieces of battered fish, all floating merrily along in the general tide of effluent pouring along London's streets. A fully self-governing ecosystem; the stuff flowed along the streets, down the drains, along the sewers, into the filtration plants, along the pipes, into people's homes, out through the taps, through the people, down the toilets, along the sewers.

A man lay in the doorway of a pub. The pub looked like it hadn't been open for a hundred years, but then a door opened and there was an oblong of smoky yellow light, a shout, a flurry of music, and someone staggered out. There might even have been other people in there, putting stuff into their mouths. There was thick grime round the edge of the door; it looked as if both door and wall were moulded from the same bit of plasticine. The windows looked like they were green, underneath the brown.

The man seemed to be asleep. A trickle of urine ran out of the bottom of his trouser leg and along the pitted tarmac. The urine found its way towards the drain by instinct. Reflected in it was the moon, broken up into little fragments by the roughness of the road, glowing.

I took a photograph of the man. His mouth was open slightly. He wore a brown suit that was too big for him. His partly closed eyes did not react to the flash of the camera.

Andi, standing vaguely in the dark, smoking her cigarette, said 'I've just been asked by two guys how much I charge.' On her own, leaning against a lamp-post waiting while I took the photo, I suppose it was an error the opportunistically-minded might make, although she was hardly dressed for the occasion. The only visible flesh was on her face.

'What did you say to them?' I asked.

'I told them that I was fine about kinky stuff, but that even I drew the line at bestiality.'

'And what did they say?'

'They sort of looked at each other, and seemed to work out that I was answering in the negative. Then they fucked off.'

Two young men lay propped against a doorway twenty feet away. I nodded towards them. 'What about them for a picture?' I said.

Andi didn't answer.

Both unshaven, both smoking cigarettes, both with empty bottles of strong beer rolling around their feet.

Clichéd image, but somewhat reduced by the fact that both were wrapped in brand new, bright pink sleeping bags. The men looked as if they were rather self-conscious about these pink puffy tubes. They'd tried putting dirty old blankets over them, to cover them up a bit, but hadn't really succeeded. The swollen pink areas of the bags emerged from the edges of the blankets like huge mutant glow-worms, fluorescently breaking free of their muddy woollen cocoons.

I explained to the men that I was putting together portraits for an exhibition and asked if I could take photographs of them. Neither of them objected. 'Good idea,' the first one said. 'How would you like us? What sort of expressions would you like us to make?'

As he asked me the question, the other one climbed out of his sleeping bag and started to roll it up.

'Er, no special kind of expression,' I replied. 'Just as you are.'

Second one. 'I don't think we should be seen in these,' he said, pointing to his bag. The first one agreed.

'Don't make anything different,' I said. 'I want this to be a photograph of things as they are, you know.'

' "Things as they are"?' repeated the second one. 'What does that mean?'

'It means I don't want you to do anything special for the camera. I want you to be how you look.'

'And how do we look?'

'Well – ' I shrugged. What did he mean by this? 'You look like homeless people,' I said. 'That's why I'm taking the picture. You're representative.'

They didn't say anything. One of them raised an eyebrow until I told him not to; he didn't have raised eyebrows when I found them. I took some pictures.

Andi stood a few feet away, shrouded in cigarette smoke, looking down the street.

'We've only just been given these sleeping bags,' the second one said.

'I do usually shave, actually,' said the first one. 'I can get razors you know. I don't think you should take photographs of me unshaven. It looks like I don't have any self-respect.'

The second one shook his head. 'We don't want to be clean-shaven,' he said. 'People will look at the photographs and think, they're all right, they're clean-shaven, we don't need to do anything to help them. That's why I don't want to be seen with these sleeping bags.'

The first one was shaking his head now. 'I don't want help from complete strangers anyway. I do have some pride, actually,' he said. 'I don't want to look like I spend my whole life sleeping in doorways. What if my mum sees it?'

'Does she go to photographic exhibitions?' I asked.

'Not as a rule.'

Click. 'Do we get copies?' the first one asked. 'Yes – er,' I said, rubbing my nose thoughtfully.

The second one grinned. 'He was about to ask us for our address,' he said. I took some more pictures.

I tucked Zoë into bed. Andi hovered in the doorway playing idly with Zoë's mobile of stars and planets.

Zoë pointed to a toy on the bedside table. 'Take it away,' she said in a small voice. 'I can't sleep with it. It's scary.'

Andi picked it up. 'It's just an elephant,' she said. 'It's a nice elephant.' She waved it in front of Zoë's face, making it bob up and down.

'It's a lion,' I told Andi quietly.

She looked more closely. 'You're right. It is a lion.' She held the toy in front of Zoë. 'It's just a lion,' she said. 'It's a nice lion.' She waved it about, making it jump up and down.

'It's still scary,' said Zoë. 'I can't sleep.'

Andi put the lion next to the photo of Yoko Ono in the living room. 'Frighten her instead,' she whispered to the lion.

Yoko looked out of the photograph with a big wide smile.

I left the strips of negatives hanging above the bath to dry. The ones with the men in their sleeping bags, I don't really think are any good. They don't *present* themselves to the viewer the way they should. It's because as soon as I told the men what my intentions were, the photographs changed somehow. They became different.

The photograph of the man pissing himself, though, is excellent. There's something in the shape of his eyes; something in the angle his shoulders are slumped at. And the way the moon reflects in the urine.

'The exhibition opens next week. My sculpture will be there,' said Andi.
'Fabulous.'
'Will you come to the opening?'
'Of course I will,' I said. 'I love openings. I'd go to the opening of a new toilet.' I'm sure I was quoting somebody but I can't remember who. It might be Wilde, or Woolf or Wittgenstein. Someone beginning with a W. It doesn't matter anyway, because Andi didn't say anything. If no one else knows I am quoting, and I can't remember who I'm quoting, it doesn't matter who said it. I might as well have made it up myself. Perhaps I did. I'm beginning to forget whether I was quoting someone and I've just forgotten who, or whether I'm trying to remember whether it's actually a quote or not. It sounds very familiar, so I think it must be a quote. But perhaps it just seems familiar because I've been thinking about it for the last few minutes. Perhaps it's my own quote after all. I've even forgotten now what it was I said, it's so long ago.

I gave the joint back to Andi. 'Thursday eight o'clock,' she was saying. 'It's black tie, so for God's sake don't turn up in a sweater like you did to the last one.'

'I was wearing a black tie underneath the sweater.'

She looked at her watch, and stubbed out the joint in the ashtray. 'Anyway, I've had a very taxing day,' she said, 'so now I'd like you to fuck me, please, hard.'

I fucked her hard.

Zoë woke up in the middle of the night and stood in the doorway, asking to be taken to the toilet. Her hair was sticking up from her head and her nightdress was caught up around her waist.

I told her she could go to the toilet on her own now, but she said she was frightened. I turned all the lights on and took her to the toilet. She sat there for a few minutes, clutching the sides of the bowl, swinging her legs over the edge. Then she said she didn't really need to go.

Lying in her bed that night under a fluffy elephant and the stars and the planets, Zoë dreamt of a large, shadowy something creeping up behind her. She didn't know what it was, but she couldn't get away from it. Every time she ran as fast as she could, it caught up with her.

present:

Everything at the opening is pink. The walls, the ceiling, the tables. There are pink glasses with rosé wine in them, pink paper plates with smoked salmon in pink sauces. The rococo lamp shades are white with red bulbs in. One wall has been left unpainted, but there's a pot of pink paint on the floor and as people pass by they dip the brush into the paint. Over the course of the evening the wall becomes pink.

I try not to think about the fact that the place looks like a cheap brothel, but I can't. Particularly as the first two women I see on entering are dressed solely in black PVC knickers with transparent pink nighties over the top. I ask Andi whether the women are for sale. Andi tells me that they're not, but that their polystyrene busts of infamous world dictators are.

The paintings have all been put into pink frames, which must be galling for some of the artists, especially if they've painted something they regard as serious. There is no serious atmosphere here. I wouldn't want the photographs I'm doing at the moment put into pink frames. Although, well, maybe the one of pink sleeping bags would look okay.

Andi takes me to her sculpture. She's quite satisfied with the way it's been presented, but I'm not sure about the pink curtains that it's backed with. I make the mistake of saying so, because she is demanding an opinion and I can't think of anything else to say.

'What do you mean?' she demands, pointing the stem of her empty wine glass at me like a pistol.

'Well – they seem a bit *drapey* to me. Look at this lovely sculpture and haven't we arranged attractive cloths behind it?'

Andi's sculpture is raw. It's a woman lying on her back staring at you. She seems to be saying, 'I don't care if you can see straight up my cunt. I'm lying like this because I want to. I'm not changing my comfortable position just because of what *you* might be able to see.'

Such is the intensity of her stare that few observers dare look down there, in case the sculpture were to get up and punch them. Everyone stands around peering dutifully at her face, talking loudly about how confidently the shape of the jaw has been moulded, that kind of thing. Andi fills her glass up from a passing girl who appears to be wearing a blancmange.

'She's a sort of guerrilla for women,' Andi says, thinking aloud. I can always tell when she is drinking on top of speed; normally she is quiet and will only express an opinion if you force it from her. 'Men always think they're sexual soldiers, don't they, with their great big phallic cannons, and missiles, that sort of thing. Men see making love as declaring war. Sex is staking out your territory and then dropping a bomb on your target. Orgasming is the bomb going off. This woman's cunt is the gaping hole that the man's bomb has left behind.'

'Right. She's not very happy about it, is she?'

'Of course she's fucking not happy about it.'

I suggest to Andi that she should have called the sculpture 'Andi's War Hole'. Andi laughs hysterically, dropping her glass and sending wine and broken glass flying everywhere. She punches me heavily in the side of my arm, telling me not to make her laugh when she has drink in her mouth. The blancmange comes back and unobtrusively clears up the debris.

A couple overhear us. They're both very pretty. Both wear identical thick blue velvet suits with bright lilac paisley ties. They look very fetching, despite the uncanny resemblance to a pair of sofas.

'Did you do this?' the woman asks Andi. 'I really like it.'

'Thanks.'

'What's it mean?'

'It means what you want it to mean,' says Andi. She studies the woman with hard eyes, wondering why she's asked the question. We know the couple have been listening to what we've been saying.

'What would you like it to mean?' the man asks Andi.

'I've spent too long wanting it to be finished,' replies Andi. 'Now that it is, I don't have anything else to say about it.'

'If it's finished,' says the woman, 'how can it mean what we want it to mean? It must be incomplete, if the audience has a part to play.' Andi's expression of contempt softens.

'If it's finished,' continues the woman, 'all we've got to do is work out what your intentions were. That's why I asked you what it was meant to mean. If it can mean what I want it to mean, it isn't finished.'

Conversations with Magic Stones

The blancmange is back so we take more pink wine. Andi sips slowly.

A sculpture of a woman on a pink plinth. It looks like it's made of plastic, but then it moves. I nearly leap about three feet, but I'm so pissed by now that my brain has worked out what it is before my relaxed muscles can react the way they want to.

The woman is naked, except for strips of black masking tape which have been stuck over apparently random parts of her body. Her arms are covered up, but her legs are bare. Her genitals have tape across them, but her breasts and bottom are exposed. There are thin strips of tape across her stomach, making her front look a bit like a wasp that has dyed its yellow parts pink.

She has baggage labels tied to the exposed areas of her body. The labels have prices written on them in felt-tip. £8,000 on her bottom. £3,000 on her thighs. £11,000 on her breasts. Lots of other labels. I don't read them all. I don't want it to look like I'm examining her carefully in order to get close to her body.

She's gazing into space vacantly, ignoring anyone who comes near. Her eyes are like a robot's, her expression is completely set. Even her skin looks unreal, shiny. What's she meant to be? The artificial woman, in a society that doesn't recognise real people? A person whose only individuality comes from where you stick bits of tape, otherwise we're all the same? Something like that. Some comment about inventing yourself by use of clothes, otherwise we're all robots. That would account for the plasticky look.

What do the price tags mean? How you can't give value to something as priceless as life? How one part of a body is worth more to society than another, even though all parts should be the same? How much you have to pay if you want to have a sexual experience with each part of her body? But those areas are naked; if she'll willingly display them for nothing, what does she do with them when she charges you that kind of money? I tap my teeth against my wine glass.

She has a perfect figure; she's very beautiful. And at the same time, strangely hideous.

I look in Andi's brochure. Apparently the woman has spent £50,000 on plastic surgery. I look up at her again and it all becomes clear. That's why her face looks so plasticky (£15,000 spent on different parts of it, almost half of that figure on various operations on her nose.) That's why she looks like a robot. That's why she looks beautiful but unattractive. Whatever is on the surface, is all.

Why has she done it? Is she a work of art? Everything about her has been sculptured, so I suppose she must be.

Two men walk up. 'Are we allowed to touch it?' one of them says. 'You're not meant to touch works of art, are you? In case you leave fingerprints on them, or something.'

'I think this is inter-active art,' says the second. 'I think you can touch it if you want to. I'm not sure if it'll react. Sometimes,' he adds knowledgeably, 'they'll respond to you, answer your questions, that kind of thing. Other times they'll completely ignore you.'

'I see,' says the first one. He clears his throat. 'Excuse me,' he asks the woman. 'Are you a piece of interactive art, or will you ignore me if I ask you a question?'

The woman doesn't say anything. The man waits patiently, hoping she'll tell him. Eventually he turns to the second guy. 'She's not answering me,' he says. 'Does that mean she's not a piece of inter-active art, or does it just mean that she's ignoring me?'

The second man is looking at the price tags and trying to work out what they mean. 'I don't know,' he says absently. 'Why don't you ask her?'

'She's got a bit of paper stuck to her ear,' the first man says. 'Perhaps that means she can't hear me. Or that she's not *meant* to be able to hear me.' He flicks through his catalogue. 'It doesn't say anything here about touching her.'

'That's very easily tested,' says the second man. He touches her neck, from a distance. Nothing happens. Then he touches her face, and her legs, and her back. Still the woman is impervious. He gets a bit braver and touches her breasts and her taped genitals.

'Evidently you are allowed to,' he concludes, stepping back and breathing heavily.

'What makes you so sure?'

'Someone would come up and tell us if we weren't.'

'She's just an object,' I say to Andi.

'Isn't that what anyone becomes, after you've turned them into a work of art?' Andi replies.

>everyone here is as unique as the next person

My head is spinning. I've drunk gallons of rosé wine. Andi is still drinking but it is not having much effect now, because of the speed she took after dinner.

I've never really had a taste for rosé wine before but it's surprising how it grows on you after eight or nine glasses. Except that I've been going to the toilet all evening. Every time I get up to go, Andi looks at me with envy. Andi likes going to the toilet. She says she likes the sense of letting go. I tell her to drink some more wine.

I like the sense of release as well, especially when I'm looking for an excuse to escape the people at our table. I wouldn't mind experiencing a sense of release all over them. For a group of people trying desperately hard to be unconventional, I suspect that standing up and pissing in front of them would make them all scream with horror. Perhaps I should try it. Make a point.

ass for ass sake

At the end of the evening Andi is given an award for her work. She's won best newcomer, or something. I go up to collect the award with her.

I look around the hall. Interpretations of black-tie vary widely. Clothes with lots of feathers, or dresses that split open in unlikely places. Men in wraparound skirts and make-up. No-one's wearing dinner jackets with bow ties, except for two women at the back.

Andi tells everyone she's very grateful, and didn't expect to win, and has really enjoyed the exhibition, and really feels part of an exciting new cultural movement, etc. etc.

She says that when you're part of a new movement, you don't really know what to call yourself. It's only after the movement has been and gone, that people can give it a label. It was only after the sixties had ended, that people were able to look back on themselves wearing black and having cropped haircuts and say, 'we were part of the Beat Generation.'

People in the fifth century didn't say to each other, 'Ooh, we're about to enter the Dark Ages. Sounds a bit scary, I don't think I want to do *that*.'

Something only exists when it has a name. If you don't give something a name until it's ended, then it can't exist for you at the time. Andi says she wants her movement to have a name now, so that it definitely exists and she's definitely there in it.

'What do you think we should call this movement?' she asks rhetorically. 'We need a name. Like the Bloomsbury Set.'

I suggest the Loganberry Set.

'Or the Raspberry set,' offers Andi. 'Because anyone who doesn't like what we're doing, well – we just fart in their faces. Our movement is all about – letting go.'

the concept of originality was someone else's idea

We get back to Andi's flat at five a.m. Brian the babysitter opens the door.

'She's fast asleep, but she woke up about an hour ago,' he says. 'She'd been having a nightmare. Something big and black had been creeping up behind her. I sat with her for a while, and told her everything was all right. She soon fell asleep again.'

Brian the babysitter goes home. I look in on Zoë. She's waving her arms around in her sleep, as if trying to pull something towards her. Or push something away.

movements have moved on

Andi's got pretty excited by how well the exhibition went. She's still high from the speed and the pink wine. She appears at the studio doorway swaying slightly, wearing a pink T-shirt and pink knickers and a huge lipsticked smile. Pink. My stomach turns a little and the last litre or so of wine sloshes around inside it. I never want to see pink ever again.

I walk over and insist she takes all the pink stuff off. When she refuses, still smiling, I rip the pink T-shirt down the middle. She falls on the floor. I pull the pink knickers away from her struggling legs. The knickers get wrapped around her feet so that when she tries to stand up, she falls over again. We struggle and push each other into the bedroom.

She's put pink sheets on the bed. I've never turned the lights off before at times like this, but now I think I might have to. She pushes herself on top of me and I can smell her skin against my face. She presses against me from all directions. Different parts of her push hard against me at different moments, and then relax. It's like the feel of a hot water bottle. You push one part down and another bit springs up somewhere else.

'Did you enjoy the exhibition?' I ask. Her neck and breasts, bottom and thighs are warm. Her feet, shoulders, fingers are cold.

'Mmm,' she murmurs. 'A professor of something or other, over here for a week, told me that when he was in Tunisia, a man with a big moustache offered him five hundred camels for his wife.'

I push up against her. She lifts herself up against me and I kiss her belly button, the skin just above her pubic hair, her hips. 'What was his answer?' I ask.

'He said if he was offered seven hundred he'd think about it.' She puts her hands on my shoulders and presses down hard. I feel her knuckles cracking.

'What did the Tunisian man do?' I lick inside her thighs. Some sweat forms there and I lick it up.

I can feel her moist hair against my eyebrows. It's so exciting it seems she's stimulating me, not the other way round. I can feel the blood pushing up along my erection, trying to force its way through the top. If I wasn't pushing my prick hard against the bed, squeezing it tight, I'd have come already. My head is spinning. I feel like I am coming, constantly.

'He offered the professor nine hundred camels, and the professor got divorced at Christmas. He left his job at Oxford and moved out there.' She goes rigid in the bed. Her legs stick out like branches from a tree. I try to lift her up so that I can feel her bottom while I'm licking her, but she's firmly clamped against the bed.

'What's he doing there?' I ask her, pushing my tongue into the folds of her skin.

'He's selling camels.' She's gasping now, making a high-pitched noise every time she breathes.

'You believe this story do you?' I ask. She ignores me. 'I want to let go,' she mutters.

'You can let go,' I say, getting even more excited because I know what this means. I push myself further into her. 'Do what you like.'

She goes very still and very quiet, then a few drops of piss emerge from her. I lick them up from where they land glistening on her hair. The piss tastes salty and is not as hot as I expected it to be. It doesn't taste at all unpleasant. Andi pisses more heavily. It runs over my face, down my neck, off my chest, onto the bed. The pink sheets start to soak, and turn a much more attractive shade of red.

I turn her over, and bury my head in her. My face is wet from her and I can't tell by now what's piss and what's sweat. I hold a buttock in each hand and gently pull them apart. I push my tongue inside her; she moves her hips back and groans. I hold her firmly apart and her flesh goes white.

I can feel the groan vibrating through her body. By now I'm not really thinking about what I'm doing; I'm somewhere between my head and the ceiling. My ears pound, even though the room is silent.

We eventually roll away and fall onto the floor, where we stay because the bed is so wet. It's already getting light outside; I pull some spare sheets from the cupboard. I dry Andi's legs in a thick fluffy towel and she rubs another towel over me. We wrap ourselves up in the sheets, kiss each other lightly on the mouth, and go to sleep.

Waking up at about nine, trapped in Andi's pink sheets, I have a flashback to the sleeping bags the men were wrapped up in at St. Pancras. Andi says they'd made her think of enormous, smothering strait-jackets. Zipped up in one of those, not only would you not be able to move your arms, but you wouldn't be able to move your legs either.

She expands on this theme, claiming that the reason the 'strait-bags' are bright pink is to persuade people to get into them in the first place. 'Here you are,' the nice doctors would say. 'Lovely colourful sleeping bags for you.' The inmates would get in, then zip! Zip! A long zip along the side. Round the corner, then zip! up the edge. A furious head sticking out of the top, veins pushing against its forehead, eyes swivelling round like a slug's stalks.

'Or,' Andi concludes, 'perhaps they're body-bags for clowns.'

I don't think I'm going to use any of those photos of the homeless. I can't think of a suitable way to present them.

'Do you want some orange juice?' I ask, as I try to struggle out of the web of pink sheets. The sun is trying to squeeze through the blinds. It's a beautiful day outside. Andi's award lies on the floor, embedded in a pink pillow. Parts of its bronze engraving are already starting to go green, because it's been pissed on.

future:

masque

I

My mother has made me act since I was five. The first thing I did was at a street festival in Rouen. I remember having to wear a mask with the face of a boy on it, and it felt very strange, pretending to be something I am not. When I had the mask on, no one knew who I was. I was disguised and could do what I liked; I didn't have to worry about being me.

The coach jolts and I open my eyes. The countryside is still flat and green but we cannot be more than an hour away from Paris. We have left far behind the houses of my village. I remember the green gates, the oval windows in the roofs, the brown shutters. I've never felt affection towards home but now I'm not there any more, I miss it.

I feel a nervousness tightening in my stomach. I don't know what Paris will be like. Across the aisle from me, Mme. Renard is still asleep, despite the noise from the tape recorder at the back. Her hands clutch her carton of apple juice, which has fallen over in her lap and let juice dribble over her fingers. The atmosphere in the coach is hot and sticky. We have been travelling for nearly three hours and the old people at the front of the coach with me are asleep.

Smoke reaches me from the back. The young members of the cast are dancing between the seats and many of them are drunk. I turn round in my seat and look at them. Philippe is dancing holding a bottle of wine. Claude is drinking vodka from the bottle. Bruno stares out of the window, cigarette burning away in his hand. The tape recorder is on at full volume and occasionally distorts, sounding as if it will split open.

There are apartments painted strangely in camouflage greens and greys, as if a graffiti artist has been allowed a free hand with the whole block. There are offices painted silver and grey. As the coach moves past them, different vertical rows of windows reflect the sunlight. We swoop into an underpass and as we emerge, between buildings I glimpse the Eiffel Tower.

– Look, young girl, shouts Claude from the back of the coach. <Your first sight of Paris. What do you think?>

I nod and smile. The Eiffel Tower has an enormous illuminated orange digital clock attached to its middle. It doesn't read the time, but it has a kind of countdown.

– That's the Millennium clock, says Claude. <It's counting down to the year 2000. Not long to go now. When it hits zero, the tower's going to take off and disappear into orbit. It's actually a rocket, you see. After two hundred years its true purpose will be revealed.>

I gaze out of the window. One of the actresses comes from the back of the coach and sits in the vacant seat next to me.

– Have you ever been to Paris before? she asks. I shake my head.

– Are you looking forward to it? She smiles at me. She has long dark hair, olive skin, green eyes. She looks friendly. She

Conversations with Magic Stones

waits for me to speak. Most people, when I don't answer them, go on to say something else, or get impatient with me. This woman just nods encouragingly, and waits for me.

– Well, I say, eventually. <I'm a little nervous.>

– That's okay, she says. <Everyone's nervous, the first time they come to the city. I think it's very brave of you. To come so far without your family, or anyone you know.>

– My mother says it will be good for me.

– Well, says the woman. <Perhaps she's right. So, my name is Adele.>

– I'm Marie, I say. <It's good to meet you,> I add.

– How old are you, Marie? asks Adele.

– Sixteen.

Adele looks out of the window. She shakes her head. <What I'd give to be sixteen again.> I expected her to say that, and I expected her to look out of the window and shake her head while she said it. It's the way people behave in films. I think people have seen so many films by the time they get older that they start to behave in film-like ways when they say certain things.

– How old are you? I ask. She tears her face away from the window and looks at me. Her face is pale and crossed by bumping, blurring shadows.

She shrugs. <Twenty-nine. That must seem incredibly old to you.>

I think for a moment. <It is quite old,> I say. <But not incredibly so,> I add, reassuringly.

We are on an immensely long straight road now, and in the distance I can see the Arc de Triomphe. It looks pale blue, virtually grey, like in a painting, as it is so far away.

– Is this the Champs d'Elysées? I ask, waving my hand at the road.

– No, answers Adele. <It doesn't become the Champs

d'Elysées until we've gone past the arch.>

I watch the arch getting nearer and nearer. I look at the restaurants and shops around us. A woman dashes between cars, clutching her scarf to her chest. In front of us, cars swerve and pirouette without indicating. A build-up of cars trying to turn left causes the coach to lurch out halfway into the slow lane to get past them.

    – I'd love to be sixteen again, says Adele. <Imagine all the boys you'll meet.>

    I shake my head. <I hardly think so,> I say.

    Adele turns to look at me. <What? Of course you will, a pretty young thing like you. The Parisian boys will leap on top of you.>

    I look at her uncertainly. <Do you think so?>

    She squeezes my arm. <You won't know what's hit you,> she says.

II

We go to our pensions first to deposit our bags, have a shower, have a drink. I am billeted at the same place as Guy, Philippe, Lisette and Ella, but I have a room to myself as there is no other girl of my age in the *troupe*.

    I sit by the balcony although I do not open the large windows. I look down on the busy street below me. I do not know which part of Paris I am in. All I know is that we got here about ten minutes after we passed under the Arc de Triomphe. Two people are arguing on a corner, waving their hands about filmically. I feel wide awake and very tired, all at the same time. I have to keep opening my eyes wide to take it all in, my mouth feels dry and I have a strange, upside-down feeling. I feel that if I move too sharply I will fall over.

I listen to brakes squealing and the occasional thump of a car stereo as it passes underneath me. The room seems very empty; it has no identity. The constant rush of traffic outside gives the room its only sound. It smells of furniture polish.

I have not been able to eat anything all day, and now I feel tired and uncomfortable as a result. But the idea of food makes me ill. I listen to my own voice rattling around my head. It seems to be made up of lots of different voices, all trying to talk at once.

The Centre Culturel Charles Baudelaire is on the corner of a side street. A couple are having an argument in the road when we first walk round the corner. It is as if they are there for my benefit, to convince me this is Paris, to provide colour. I imagine the camera sweeping past them and homing in on me as I walk towards the theatre; then the two extras will stop acting and wander off for a coffee.

The theatre is an old building with walls of flaking plaster, like icing on a wedding cake after people have been nibbling at it. The small blue road plate has been nailed on neatly, and newly lacquered bright red wooden signs have been put directly onto the crumbling masonry. The front of the building has been almost completely replaced with a huge glass window, with a door built directly into the glass. Posters of our production have been put up above the window. Next to the theatre is a jazz club, with black windows sunk into grey stone.

There are lots of leaflets about our play on the wooden counter in the foyer. I take one and put it in my bag. It seems odd, taking a leaflet as if I am an audience member when in fact I'm in the play. I look around, but no one is watching me.

I go up and have a look at the stage. It is shrouded in darkness, one or two large fresnels giving the stage a dim, cavernous appearance. It is reasonably large. Seats come down to it on three sides. I am surprised at how dirty the stage is. It is covered in old bits of tape, all different colours, and the stage is so filthy it is more grey than black. There is an old wooden table in the middle of the stage and a hat stand.

III

That night the theatre has organised a reception party for the cast and crew. We are in some kind of function room, at the back of the theatre, divided by a bar into two smaller rooms.

Trestle tables line the walls, piled high with food. Thick slices of ham stacked up against each other. Bowls of button mushrooms in a rich tomato sauce. Thin slices of raw bacon, red and translucent like sweet wrappers. Salami and tomato slices arranged into the shape of a butterfly.

I cut a small piece of cheese, then feel myself going red as I realise I've used the wrong knife. No one seems to have noticed though; everybody is too busy talking to everybody else. They wave their hands and lift their heads up to drop salami into their mouths. One strange man with a red beard has black eyebrows that shoot up and down as he talks. People circle around one another. Everyone seems to know everyone else. In the corner of the room, Mme. Renard is sitting in a chair asleep, her head on one side, her hands folded in her lap.

Conversations with Magic Stones

A young man of about twenty comes up to me. I vaguely recognise him from the coach. He offers me a bowl of radishes. I hesitate, then take one. He smiles as I study the radish; I've never eaten one before. I pull the green bit off, as I imagine you're supposed to do that, then I put the radish in my mouth and bite. My head feels hot and I nearly choke. The man laughs and touches me on the back.

– Look, he says. He takes a radish, slices it lengthways, covers it in butter and tips salt on it. He takes a small bite.

– My name's Antoine, he says. I nod. <Would you like another radish?> I shake my head. He touches my back again, leaning down towards me. His breath is hot and smells of garlic, onions, exotic things. Behind him, I see Adele. She's looking at me with her eyebrows slightly raised, as if to say, I told you so. She smiles, then turns her back on us to pick some food from the table.

Suddenly the lights go off. I panic, thinking there's a fire or a flood or something. No one else seems worried though. After a second there's an ear-splitting noise which doesn't stop but keeps going, in pulsating thumps like an alarm.

It takes me a moment to realise that it is music. When I walk into the other room, I see that the tables have been cleared. Already there are people dancing. I look around the room.

At one end is a huge photograph of a battle in a large gilt frame. Something seems wrong about the photograph but I cannot tell what it is. As I am thinking about it I become aware of a presence next to me. <Hello? Hello?>

It is Antoine. He asks me to dance. I look at him.

– Oh, go on, he says.

I think about it. I don't think I'd be very good and I don't want to embarrass myself; but Antoine holds me by the waist and propels me into the middle of the room. <I know you won't say anything,> he says. <So I'll just have to take your silence as acceptance.>

We dance. Antoine holds me close to him and I can smell his aftershave. Every time he moves, his hair drops a necklace of beads of sweat onto his collar. He looks at me from time to time but the room is very dark and I cannot read his face properly. As he dances he grunts with the exertion. His tie is loose and he is covered in sweat. Now his breath smells of salami and cheese.

He pulls me towards a corner of the room. Other people dance around us in a blur. He has his hands round my waist and occasionally it slips onto my bottom. He does this very artfully, trying to make out that it is the motion of the dancing that is making him occasionally lose his grip on my waist. He thinks I will not notice what he is doing.

In the corner, he stops abruptly, puts his wet hand on my face and tries to kiss me. The smell of salami and sweat pours into my throat. I reel back from him instinctively as he paws me and attempts to put his tongue in my mouth. I feel myself shudder. He detects this shudder and backs away from me.

I imagine that he will be terribly cross with me, but he isn't. He just smiles and takes his arm away from my waist. <See you later,> he says, and he wanders off into the other room, where the drink is.

I go over to the corner and stand on my own. The DJ glances up at me then goes back to his records. I look at the photograph of the battle. It is a very detailed photo; there are hundreds of people fighting. I realise what it was that struck me as wrong about it. It is a photograph of the French Revolution.

I think about this for a moment. How can there be a photo-

graph of the French Revolution? Surely that took place long before photography was invented? Perhaps it's a historical re-enactment. Perhaps it's not the French Revolution after all. I look closely; I think it is. The costumes, certainly, seem older than nineteenth-century.
I realise eventually that it's not a photograph. It's a painting. It's so detailed, so accurate, it just looks like a photograph, even when I am this close to it. I am very impressed. It must have taken the artist an extremely long time.

IV

The afternoon of the dress rehearsal we all get there early. Most of the cast go to the bar. Antoine asks me to come for a drink with them but I say I want to run through my lines. I go for a walk backstage. The only illumination comes from a couple of small strip-lights, covered in blue plastic. The lights make everything look ghostly and mysterious.
I stand behind the flats and look up above me. The flies are incredibly high. I have to lean backwards to be able to look directly upwards. It makes me dizzy. Like looking up into the sky at night and feeling that you will fall over because you're looking so far away. You have to look down again to realise you're safely on firm ground.
In the narrow passageway backstage there is a huge trestle table set out with all the props for the performance. Each prop has its shape drawn on the table in white pen, like the way you see positions of bodies marked out on floors in crime films.
Past the table there is a set of wooden steps leading down to the dressing rooms. There are five or six steps, then a little platform, then the steps go in the opposite direction for another five

or six steps under the stage. There's a square formed by the change of direction like a box without a lid on it. It makes a kind of cubby-hole.

I clamber on top of the wooden banister and jump into the box. There is enough room to sit down and all I can see above me is the high ceiling. Unless you actually looked into the box you wouldn't know I was there.

I lean back in my little cubby-hole for a while. There is a strong smell of damp wood. I listen to strange, disembodied noises on the stage and wonder what they are. Someone sweeping up, perhaps. Someone moving small pieces of furniture. I sit there until I lose sense of time. I start to doze. I listen idly to the noises around me without trying to interpret them.

I climb out of the cubby-hole and walk down the little steps to the dressing room. No one else has come down yet. The dressing room is directly underneath the stage and I can hear the muffled noise of something being dragged across it.

There is just one large dressing room. There's a little bathroom and shower installed unusually in the middle of the room. Some of the older members of the cast are outraged that they do not have separate dressing rooms, but the theatre is very small. I am realising that this company is not a very important one. I have been told by the cast that it is important, but I think that is just because they like to think it is. Here we are, we are in a tiny theatre in a backstreet of Paris and we are only doing five performances; we are hardly the *Théâtre de la Huchette*.

I look round the room. Some people have evidently been down and adopted little areas of the room already. Mme. Renard has put postcards of paintings by Monet and Renoir above her mirror. There are good luck cards pinned to the surrounding walls. One of her necklaces dangles over the edge of the sink.

I move my bag to an unoccupied corner. I take some stuff out and litter it on the dressing table the way the others have done, so that it looks like a properly taken space. I go to turn on a light but when I press the switch the whole set of lightbulbs around each of the mirrors all comes on at once. I squint in the sudden, overpowering light.

From somewhere upstairs I can dimly hear music playing, then stopping, then the same short passage of music being repeated. It's still very early but I decide to get changed. I don't want anyone to see me without my clothes on. I get dressed and then sit in my corner. I am very nervous, although I could never admit this to the principals. They would just think, what's she got to be nervous about? She's only got two lines.

Antoine walks in to the dressing room.

– Oh no! he exclaims. He stands in the doorway, his arms folded. <The beautiful girl has got changed already! I thought I would be early enough. But it seems I am too late.> He walks over to me with a grin on his face. I smile a little at him. He notices this smile, catches it like it is something I have thrown at him and walks over with it, weighing it in his hands.

He pulls a chair up and turns it round so that its back is to me. He sits on it backwards, his legs splayed out either side so he looks like a theatre director in a film, though I have never seen a theatre director in a theatre sit like this. He leans close to me and whispers into my ear. Onions and vodka today. <She is so quiet, the beautiful girl,> he says. <She never says a word.> He shakes his head.

I shake my head.

Antoine laughs. Two more actors come into the dressing

room; Claude and someone whose name I don't know. Antoine lifts a finger up and points it at me. <By the end of the week,> he says, <I will have you talking and laughing as loudly as everyone else.>

He rubs a hand through my hair and you can see the muscles under his skin. Then he pulls his T-shirt over his head and throws it on the floor. He has very brown skin. He stands by the costume rail, humming to himself, looking for his clothes.

V

The evening of the first performance. The stage manager is running round with wires trailing from her head as if she is a robot. I wonder if anyone will trip over her wires, as they are snaking over the entire backstage area. She wears an expression of permanent anxiety. When I lift something off the props table to have a look at it, she shouts at me to put it back immediately. I shrug at her and put it back. She comes over and inspects it, as if I might have irretrievably damaged it by picking it up, then nods curtly and walks away clutching her head, a cable trailing obediently behind her.

I sit in my little cubby-hole, waiting for the play to begin. I hear lots of people running about, setting props on stage, giving calls to the actors in the dressing rooms, banging hammers into things, flapping scripts. No one can see me where I am and no one worries about where I am either. As I'm not on until the second half I don't get a call until the interval. I can sit in here and feel perfectly safe. The dressing room is crammed with people and smells of sweat and make-up. I feel much better staying here.

I've worked out that in future, the best time to get changed will be just before the end of the first half. At that time, everyone else is on stage and I can get dressed in an empty room.

I hear voices getting louder as they near me, then the dim light gets even dimmer. I look up. Someone is sitting on the rim of the cubby-hole.

– Quite sweet in a way, I suppose, the voice is saying. It is Antoine.

– I don't think I've heard her speak a single word, says the other voice, which sounds as if it belongs to Claude.

– Ah, says Antoine, lowering his voice. <The quiet ones are the ones you want to watch. I have to break her out of her shyness.>

– I think you're wasting your time, says Claude.

– You wait and see, says Antoine. <I'll bet you she is a foxy minx when you get to know her. I'm going to get her to kiss me before the end of the show.>

– She's just a child, says Claude. <I don't think she's interested in that kind of thing.>

Antoine snorts. <You wait and see,> he says.

VI

During the first half, Adele finds me sitting on the steps leading down to the stage door.

– Hello, she says. She smiles.

There's a pause. She sits down next to me.

– When I was sixteen, she says, <I had my first tour. We did a season of Shakespeare plays in Lyon, and I didn't understand a word of what I was saying. I was so nervous all the time I used to be sick in the dressing room before every performance. I remember I had a beautiful green silk dress to wear every night. I used to stand under the lights on the stage and watch the

colours changing in the silk. It was the most beautiful, expensive thing I'd ever worn. I kept worrying I would throw up on it.>
    I smile at her.
    – But you don't need to worry, she says. <Everyone will look after you. Everyone's very friendly in the *troupe*.>
    I nod.
    – On the last day, she says, <we'll have a walk round Paris. Would you like that?>
    I nod.
    She lifts her head, listening to the sound of voices on stage above us. <I've got to go,> she says. <I'm on in a moment.> She runs up the wooden steps. I listen to the speeches and the occasional creaking of the ceiling.

Although we have to be at the theatre each evening by six, the whole of the day is free for us to do as we please. Usually I sit up by the balcony in my room and watch the people going past on the street below. It's funny that when I first came to the room it seemed frightening, and I didn't want to stay there and I couldn't get to sleep. Now, the room seems safe and I am pleased to get back to it and don't want to leave it.
    I enjoy watching from the window because I can see the passers-by but they can't see me. I watch one man stop in the street, backtrack a pace and look carefully on the ground. He's seen a coin or something. He pauses there for a moment, his hands on his knees, then he carries on walking without finding anything.

VII

Friday. The play ends tonight. Adele has arranged to take me into the centre of Paris this morning. She is sitting in the lobby when I come down at ten past nine. She is sitting very upright in the cane chair and smiles at me when I appear.

– Ten minutes late, she says. <That's not very good. You couldn't be ten minutes late for a stage entrance, could you?>

The concierge looks down at her books.

I walk over to her. <I don't do many stage performances at nine o'clock in the morning,> I say, my voice crackly with sleep.

She laughs and pushes her hand through my ruffled hair, trying to smooth it down. <You're a funny young girl,> she says.

We walk out of the building. <You know,> she says, <everyone else thinks you're very quiet. But we know better, don't we?>

– I am very quiet with everyone else, I say.

We walk a little way along the street then Adele beckons me towards the métro entrance. I look up at the looped, elegant wrought iron bar that arches over the stairway. The writing of the word *Métropolitain* is woven into the rest of the ironwork like the old, gnarled branches of a tree.

– That's very pretty, I say, pointing.

– It's a style called art deco, she says, as we walk down the steps. <Did you know that?>

– No, I say.

To begin with we have to stand up, but after a couple of stops some people get off and Adele secures two seats next to each other. A man tries to sit on one of them, but she shoos him away. <*C'est pour m'amie,*> she mutters quickly. I sit down. After a while the train emerges into daylight and I blink in the sun. We rattle along a track that swoops upwards and instantly we are travelling above rows of houses. It seems as if we are flying.

Adele watches me looking down. <You are frightened?> she says.

I shake my head. <Not really.>
– Are you being honest?
I shake my head. <Not really.>
– Where would you like to go? asks Adele.
I shrug. I haven't really thought about it.
– You want to go up the Eiffel Tower?
I shudder. <No,> I say emphatically. Adele laughs.
– OK. Somewhere on the ground. Perhaps Notre Dame?
– Yes, I say. <That would be nice.>

Walking along by the river, Adele stops at one of the green boxes that sit up against the wall. She looks at some books that are packed into shelves. The pages are yellow like marzipan. I jump as I notice there is a little man tucked into the corner of the box.

Old prints hang by string from the roof. Adele looks through the prints, putting her head on one side so they appear upright. I look along the Seine. The square, grey bridge looks like a vice, holding the river in place. I look up and see Notre Dame emerging from behind the trees on the far bank like a twin-headed dragon.

– I thought you were keeping up with me, says a voice in my ear. I jump.

– Sorry, I say. <I was... just looking.>

– It's entrancing, isn't it? says Adele. She stands parallel with me, folds her arms and looks up.

The cathedral gleams with a buttery, biscuity glow in the late morning light. <It looks brand new,> I say.

Conversations with Magic Stones

– It's just been restored. It used to look a dull, grey colour. Like the bridge. Now see how attractive it is?

A gorgeous, edible sandstone colour. <They must have spent lots of money on it,> I say.

– For the Millennium they are going to put two spires on it.> I frown. <Spires? What kind of spires?>

– Oh, they're going to be in keeping with the style, says Adele. <Well, apparently,> she adds. <I don't think they're going to keep them permanently. They won't be as real as the rest of the cathedral. They'll just be made to look as though they are.>

Inside Notre Dame it is cool and dark. Everyone speaks quietly and the hush of voices circulates in the air like a breeze. There are lots of tourists standing and staring. There doesn't seem to be anyone praying. About half the tourists have miniature video cameras, which as they walk around are attached to their faces like gasmasks.

– Look at this. Adele points me to an immensely long wood carving. <It's telling the story of Christ. Look,> she says. <You get the whole story. Here's the Nativity. Here's the murder of the innocents.>

I look. The carvings are very expressive, almost cartoon-like. At the far right, a man points his finger at some keen audience members, perhaps telling them a good joke. Another man in another panel points in another direction, apparently telling someone to go somewhere.

The extreme left panel shows a man holding a woman's breast. As if he is plucking an apple.

I have to look twice to see if I haven't just imagined it. It seems so out of place in a cathedral. Such a consciously sexual piece of imagery. I wonder what it means and why it's there at the head of this procession of religious tableaux.

I turn to ask Adele about it but she's wandered off. I walk towards the other end of the carving, feeling the soft air on my face like a soothing hand.

– We must get you something for tonight, says Adele.
– What's so special about tonight?
– The party after the last performance, she explains. <It's a masked ball. Do you know what that is?>
– Kind of, I say uncertainly. We are walking along a side corridor in the cathedral. Our footsteps echo on the stone floor. On our left we are suddenly hit by red and blue light. We look up to see an enormous, round stained glass window.
– It's a rose window, she says. <It used to be the largest rose window in the world,> says Adele. <But it's not any more.>
– Oh well, I say, <never mind.>
We stand for a few moments just looking at it. It is very pretty. The reds and blues flash like lights.
– Yes, anyway, says Adele. <The masked ball. Really it's just like a fancy-dress party. Except that everyone wears masks. You know. Like at the beginning of *Romeo and Juliet*. Masks that cover your eyes.>

In a cheap shop selling trinkets of the Eiffel Tower and postcards, Adele finds some masks hanging up on the door. <Look,> she says. <That's what we want.> She buys two masks. They are made of black felt and have silver thread around the edges and around the eye-holes.

She takes me for lunch in a kind of Greek fast food restaurant. The restaurant is packed with people eating salad and meat with their fingers. I wonder where we are going to sit.

The man behind the counter cuts slices of pork straight from a leg that is rotating in the window. He hands me a paper plate. The meat comes with lettuce, radishes, tomatoes, a pool of cream, and rather incongruously, chips. On top of the plate, he drops a large round slice of pitta bread. It covers the plate's contents entirely, like a lid.

– *Quarante francs*, the man says. Adele intervenes and pays for both of us.

– It's all right, I say. <I have money.> But Adele bustles me towards the back of the restaurant. <Can't have you paying,> she says. <You're supposed to be looked after.>

I see as we get to the back of the room that there is a set of wooden steps. Downstairs, the restaurant is much emptier and there are plenty of places to sit. The room is small and cavernous, with a low ceiling. The walls are painted wine red. I sit at a table in the corner and Adele joins me. There are a few specks of yellow dust on the table, and when I look up, I see that the ceiling is made of a kind of crumbling yellow stone.

I wipe the dust off the table, put my plate down, and try not to think about ceiling dust falling into my meal as I am eating.

– It's good? asks Adele. I nod. I am thinking about the glistening leg that was turning in the window upstairs, and how much it looked like a human leg, and as I think of the leg turning, my stomach turns with it.

Adele is holding the pitta bread in one hand and smearing yoghourt onto it. She picks up pieces of meat and salad and chips and drops them onto the bread, then she rolls the bread up so it is like a tortilla and bites into the end. I stop eating with my fork and copy her.

– Have you got a dress to wear for tonight? Adele asks me between mouthfuls.

I think for a moment. <I've brought an evening dress with me,> I say. <My mother said I might get asked out somewhere formal.>

– Perfect. Adele smiles at me.

We eat in silence for a few moments. <What do you think of Antoine?> Adele asks eventually.

I shrug.

– He's very keen on you, you know.

– I know.

Adele looks at me, her head bowed as she eats. A smile turns up one corner of her mouth. <He's not so bad, is he?> she asks.

– No, not so bad, I reply.

We eat in silence, chewing. The cream is sour and cool after the hot garlic in the meat.

– Are you married? I ask Adele.

She shakes her head, and draws circles with her hand while she swallows something. <No,> she says eventually. <I was. But he went.>

– Oh.

She points her knife at me. <You'd better find yourself a boy you do like,> she says. <Because we're leaving tomorrow.>

– Yes, I say.

I put the remains of my salad into the last corner of pitta bread.

VIII

Before the final performance I don't sit in my cubby-hole; I feel a bit more able to see everyone. I walk down to the dressing room. Mme. Renard is sitting on a chair by the door, dozing, a little dribble coming out of the side of her mouth.

Claude, naked to the waist, is vigorously rubbing his face with a towel. When he puts the towel down, his face is bright red and his eyes have sunk back into their sockets. His face looks very strange without glasses. He fumbles about on the dressing table, finds his glasses, puts them on and looks normal again.

Antoine notices me. <Here she is,> he says. <The girl who keeps hiding from everyone. Where have you been?>

I shrug.

Antoine laughs. <She never says anything, does she?>

Claude grins. <Perhaps she only speaks when she hears something worth responding to,> he says.

Antoine frowns. <That's not true, is it?> he asks me.

I shrug.

Adele emerges from the bathroom in the centre of the room. She still has trousers on, but on her top half she is just wearing a white lace bra. <Ah, hello, Marie,> she says, registering me. She comes over and hugs me briefly. I can smell soap on her naked arm. Her flesh is very pale. She walks over to her area of dressing table and takes her trousers off. Her panties are also of white lace. I can see through them to the dark smudge of hair underneath.

Claude and Antoine are both looking at her, not saying anything, trying to stand at right angles to her so it doesn't look like they are looking.

– Where's my dress? Adele asks abstractedly.

Claude points to one of the rails. <There.>

– Who put it there? Adele takes the dress. As she reaches to pick it up I see the haze of black in her armpit from where she has shaved. She lifts the dress down and turns her back to me. I see that her panties are those kind that only have a string for a back. I see her naked bottom, pale and full, move up and down as she walks back the few paces to the dressing table.

I sit down quietly in my corner. Adele looks across at me. <All right?> she asks me, smiling openly. I don't say anything. Antoine laughs. Adele climbs into her dress.

On stage, I stand and look out. The lights are so strong that I cannot see the audience. I know there are two hundred people there, but all I can see is blackness; it's as if there is no one.

In my costume, I am not me. I am a serving girl in fifteenth century Orleans. There is no little girl, frightened of being in Paris.

We get changed for the ball. I've never been to so many parties. I am getting bags under my eyes from so many late nights. These actors, they are so irresponsible. They do not know when it is time to go to bed, they just want to stay up all night. No wonder they work in the evenings; nobody can get up before lunchtime.

Of course, 'ball' is just a fantasy term. Some people are in fancy dress, and most are wearing masks like the ones Adele and I have, but the ball is held in the same rooms as before, and essentially it's just another party.

I have tucked myself away behind the enormous loudspeakers. They make quite a nice hidey-hole. I don't think I will stay here when they start the music though.

New people are beginning to filter in through the doors: people I don't know, or perhaps I do know them and I just don't recognise them behind their masks. I recognise Adele quickly enough because she has the same mask as me. Her hair falls behind it and onto the front of her green silk dress.

Conversations with Magic Stones

I put my mask on, stand up and emerge from between the speakers. Antoine comes up to me. He is dressed as Cyrano de Bergerac, with a huge feather dancing from a wide-brimmed hat, a ludicrous false nose and black moustaches that twitch as if trying to get away from the monstrosity above them.

He smiles. <Now little mouse,> he says. <You keep running away from me, but it's time I caught you.> He puts one hand on the hilt of his sword and the other arrestingly on my shoulder.

I raise my hands to my mouth, pretend to scream in terror and run away to the other end of the room. I stand under the painting, my hands folded in front of everybody, looking at everyone from behind my mask.

Adele is standing in the centre of the room talking to someone I don't know. The person eventually wanders off and Adele turns to look at me. I cannot tell what her expression is behind her black mask. As she walks towards me, the colours in her silk dress shift and change in the multicoloured lights. She stands in front of me. She cannot see my expression either because of my own mask.

We stand very close to each other. When I can taste her hot breath in front of me, she kisses me slowly on the mouth. We kiss leisurely. Saliva runs into my mouth and I feel my heart throbbing against my ribcage. Adele's tongue flicks over my teeth, darting between the gaps like a lizard hiding in the cracks between rocks.

I cannot see anyone else in the room because the eyeholes of my mask do not allow me to. I feel Adele's body pressing up against me. She pushes her hand into the small of my back. I shift and mould myself to the shape of her hips, her breasts.

We separate. Claude is standing at the bar holding a bottle of wine, his glasses on top of his head, scrunching his eyes up and trying to read the label on the bottle. Antoine has found a chair and has sat down squarely in front of the food table, eating directly from the dishes. Mme. Renard is asleep. No one has seen anything.

Adele takes her mask off. I take my mask off. Adele lowers her head and shakes her hair out. She looks up at me. I smile at her. She smiles back at me.

Adele's room is bigger than mine. She has a crescent-shaped balcony. I look round.

– Aren't you sharing? I ask.

– I paid extra, she says. When she closes the gold-handled door, it hardly makes a sound. I look at her. She does not say anything.

Adele steps out of her dress in one fluid movement like a butterfly emerging from a pupa. The dress slithers to the floor and swims about for a moment before coming to a rest on the soft carpet.

She turns to look at me. <You are okay?> she says.

I nod.

– Anything you need to do?

I shake my head. I open my dress. It falls away from me.

We lie together in the smooth, deep bed. Waves of her perfume reach me each time the sheets billow, each time we turn over. I do not say anything. I lie by her side, nestling into her, licking the tips of her breasts, stroking the fine hairs on her stomach.

IX

There are thunderclouds low in the sky. The air whistles through the tunnel that swoops down by the Arc de Triomphe as we travel away from the theatre. The orange lights flash against the faces of the people in the coach, lighting them up then plunging them into darkness almost as quickly as a strobe. Antoine is eating a piece of salami which he's rolled round some sliced mushrooms. Claude is drinking vodka from the bottle. Mme. Renard is asleep next to me. The heady smells of garlic and alcohol mix with the diesel from the coach, and I feel light-headed.

We emerge from the darkness and head towards the Louvre. 'That's the Madélèine on the right,' Claude says. I look, and briefly see a large grey cathedral, set back between two other, nearer buildings. 'That's where Fauré wrote his Requiem,' he adds.

As the Louvre flashes past on the left, Claude rests his vodka bottle on the vacant seat next to him. <When they were cleaning the Madélèine,> he says, <they hung a huge canvas over the scaffolding and painted a life-size copy of the front of the cathedral on it. So that anyone looking from the Place de la Concorde didn't have their view spoilt. You'd look down and there would be the Madélèine – and you'd be none the wiser. It was so perfectly painted, you'd never know you weren't looking at the real thing. You wouldn't guess the cathedral was actually buried under hundreds of tonnes of metal tubes.>

Claude shakes his head. <What a wonderful idea,> he says. <You wouldn't get that happening anywhere other than Paris.> He shakes his head again and picks up his vodka bottle.

I look around at the other buildings as they travel past me. I wonder if they are real, or just painted on.

Soon we are out of Paris, travelling back through the Bois de Boulogne, and I know that in three hours' time we will be home and all the members of the company will go their separate ways. I look down the coach. It has started to rain and the large central windscreen wiper smears backwards and forwards as the coach bumps up and down. Antoine is sitting in the seat behind me on his own, drinking wine.

He leans round in his seat and touches me on the shoulder.

– I don't live too far away from you, he says. <Perhaps we can exchange addresses. I could buy you a drink one day.>

I look at him and shrug.

He tears the label off his bottle of wine. It rips away after he's pulled half the label off, but there's room enough to write his number down.

Claude comes and stands next to him. <Ah,> he says, <the young man, still trying his best. Don't take any notice of him, will you?> he says to me.

I shrug. Antoine holds the ragged label out to me but as I am about to take it, his lip curls and he retracts his hand. He looks at me carefully for a moment, his eyes a little mournful, and then slowly he screws the thin piece of paper up and drops it amongst the cigarette butts and fluff that carpet the floor.

Claude sits next to Antoine. They talk as if I am not there.

<She is so shy,> says Antoine. <I don't suppose she has ever even kissed a boy. She is so innocent.>

– Ah, says Claude, <what it would be, to be sixteen again.> They look at each other knowingly, full of masculine worldliness. Claude clicks his teeth and winks.

I am the first to be dropped off. The coach heaves into my town and I am left at the intersection. I have two large, heavy bags, but it's only round the corner to my house. My road is one-way anyway; the coach would not get onto it.

Adele helps me down with my bag. The other people on the coach wave, then go back to their drinking. The coach chugs patiently as it waits for Adele.

– We have to stay in touch, she says. I nod. She writes her address and number down on a piece of paper and hands it to me.

I hunch my shoulders as the rain trickles down my neck. Adele wipes some wet hair out of her face. She says something but there is a blast of wind and cold rain and I do not hear what she says. She leans forward, holds my neck with her hand and kisses me on the mouth.

The wind changes direction and rain hits my face directly. Water goes into my eyes and makes them sting. Adele turns quickly and gets back on the coach, water flicking from her fast-turning head. I glance at the piece of paper in my hand. The rain has already made the blue ink run.

The doors of the coach hiss shut, the chugging increases, and it launches itself away into the road. Antoine looks out at me and puts his hand to his temple in a kind of wave, then the coach gets smaller and smaller until it turns away onto the main road. I can still taste Adele on my mouth.

I stand there, feeling myself getting smaller and smaller from the point of view of the vanishing coach, until I finally disappear.

X

I walk slowly along the narrow road. My ears are ringing with the quiet. All I can hear is the monotonous, faint rush of rain dripping down the leaves. The noises and smells of Paris keep rushing past me, making me dizzy. I try to focus on the achingly silent street again.

I reach my house and stand for a moment in front of it, looking up, wondering how it can be that nothing has changed and yet the house seems so strange to me. The shutters are down because it is such a wet day. My mother rushes out to greet me, taking my bags from me and hugging me several times. I tell her how pleased I am to see her and how I have had a wonderful time, but how I am pleased to be back home.

Upstairs, I put Adele's piece of paper on the dressing table. I unpack slowly. My evening dress is terribly crumpled, because I did not bother to pack it properly. I drop it in the corner of the room. I open the window and feel the damp breeze invade the mustiness of the disused room. The rain is easing off now.

I pull the black felt mask from my bag and look at it for a moment. I take a picture down from the wall and hang the mask on the hook and gaze at the mask. It is hanging unevenly, one eye above the other, and it seems to be looking at me thoughtfully. Weighing me up.

I pick up Adele's crumpled piece of paper and iron it out with the back of my hand. It has gone soggy and when I look at it, it is blank. I turn it over, but the other side is blank too. There is a marbled effect of pale blue ink all over the paper.

I pin the blank piece of paper on my notice board and look out of the window at the tops of the houses and the firs, and beyond them, invisible now, the city. The bland, grey light hides the sun. The mask looks down on me, its empty eye sockets staring like a skull.

also available
by mark blayney

two kinds of silence

A woman living inside a stone circle hides an unusual secret… a couple in Turkey take a boat trip to search for turtles… an elderly artist becomes obsessed with her young model… these are mystical, lyrical stories, eloquent and sophisticated.

'A perceptive storyteller of real promise'
BERYL BAINBRIDGE

Free postage and packing in the UK. To order, send a cheque for £10 per copy made payable to Manuscript Publishing to: 41 Southview Road, Marlow, Bucks SL7 3JR.
ISBN 0 9545505 1 X

Available in August 2004:

Saturnalia
A third volume of short stories

In the light of setting suns
A novel

To receive information about these books on publication, please send your email address to orders@manuscriptbooks.co.uk or include it with your order.

To read extracts visit www.manuscriptbooks.co.uk